All I Want For Christmas Is Them

ADORA CROOKS

Copyright © 2021 by Adora Crooks

Editing by One Love Editing

Book Cover by Melody Jeffries

All rights reserved.

No part of this book may be reproduced in any form or by any electronic or mechanical means, including information storage and retrieval systems, without written permission from the author, except for the use of brief quotations in a book review.

* * *

Sign up to get newsletter alerts (plus you get a free MMF romance).

Join the club 📩 https://adoracrooksbooks.com/gift

AUTHOR'S NOTE

It's been a hard couple of years for everyone, including the characters in this novel. I wanted to write a book that reflected and embraced life's challenges rather than shove them under the rug. In between crisp banter, lifelong friendships, and steamy, kindle-melting multiple partner scenes, this is a story about growing up and learning to let go.

Please be aware that this Christmas romance mentions themes of grief and parent death. If that's a bit too heavy for you, feel free to put this down until you're ready to pick it back up. Have a wonderful, love-filled time!

XOXO,

Adora

PART I

THE SHOW. DECEMBER 23RD

1

OTTO

"Close your eyes."

Naomi's eyes are beautiful. Big. Brown. Doe-like. Perfect eyebrows, which furrow now in excited puzzlement. "Why?" she asks.

"Close. Your. Eyes. Love."

At the pet name, she smiles and obeys.

I'm sure we look ridiculous right now—sitting across from each other at a rickety metal table outside of Citarella's. The table legs have snow caked to them like white moss. It's late December in Long Island, and we're crazy people for sitting outside.

But Naomi and I are also creatures of habit, and this is routine. When she spends the night with me, I take her to get coffee while we wait on the Long Island Rail Road to zip her back to the city.

I'm a stay-at-home writer, so I have time to kill. Naomi works two jobs in the city—she's a tattoo artist and a part-time barista. Put her crazy hours with our near long-distance relationship (forty-five minutes one way on the LIRR is no easy feat), we have to carve out time for each other, or else we'll never find it.

We've been dating for almost six months now, but the shine hasn't worn off. I take my time admiring her with her eyes closed. She's a bundle of faux-fur-lined navy and anticipation.

Naomi is objectively beautiful. Thick black hair so long, it falls over her breasts. Golden-brown skin. A small, button nose with a septum piercing. Wide, feminine curves.

But what's really beautiful about her—and I mean, breathtakingly stunning—is her smile. She's spent the latter part of her twenties rebelling against her conservative upbringing from her Iranian-American parents, and it shows with tattoos, piercings, and a *fuck you* swagger. She's a badass, and I can readily admit that I'd probably lose a fight with her.

But when she smiles…every wall and hard edge she'd built up over the years come crashing down. She has this sweet, innocent, Disney-princess smile that makes my heart do a barrel roll every time I see it.

I take a small box out of my coat pocket and pass it across the table to her. "Okay. Open them."

She does. She blinks down at the box. "What is this?"

"Merry Christmas."

"It's not for another two days, psycho."

"Merry *early* Christmas, then."

She squints at me and then promptly tears the top open.

She shouts and immediately closes it.

"Otto!" she says, her voice shaking with laughter. "You can't give this to me…*in public*."

I shrug. "What do you give the woman who has everything? The one thing she asks for."

She bites her plump lip. I can see the excitement dancing in her eyes.

Even in the frosty winter weather, my blood goes hot.

About two months ago, after shagging each other's brains

out, Naomi and I lay side by side in sweat-slicked sheets and pillow-talked.

"Tell me your kinkiest fantasy," I said.

Even in the dark, I could see her blush. "You're going to think it's weird."

"I promise, I won't."

"Okay. Well. I have this fantasy that I'm wearing a sex toy—like one of those remote-controlled vibrators? I'm in public, and my boyfriend keeps turning it on at inconvenient moments."

"Hot."

She'd scrunched her nose. "You think it's weird."

"No, I think it's hot."

"It's…the lack of control, I think, that turns me on." Naomi reached up and tugged her fingers through my hair. "And the thought of doing that with someone I trust."

"Are you saying you trust me?"

"Eighty-nine percent of the time."

"I'll take those odds."

That was then. This is now. Now, Naomi stares at me with the eyes of an uncaged cougar.

I want to give her everything she ever wanted.

If Naomi wants expensive earrings, I'll get them for her.

If she wants matching tattoos, I'll grin and bear it.

And if she wants to orgasm in a room full of people, then I'm damn well going to make it happen. It doesn't hurt that the thought makes my pants tight.

"You know me way too fucking well," she says.

"Wear it," I tell her. "Tonight."

The demand in my voice makes her eyes go wide. She draws her fingertips over the top of the box, teasing it.

"Otto Stratton," she says, her voice low and coy, "you're a fucking bastard."

"I know." I get up to lean over the table and press a kiss to her mouth. Her lips are warm and soft and urging against mine. "Do you love it?"

She smiles into my kiss. "I love it."

I grin. "Wicked."

2

DIEGO

I have no idea how I'm going to tell him.

I stare at the blood panel results in my hands, trying to wrap my head around it.

The results are for Otto Stratton. Otto has been my best friend since we were teenagers. But even after all that time, I still have trouble breaking bad news to him.

"Diego."

The sound of my name jerks me to attention, and I lift my eyes from the paper.

Dr. Adam Donovan is the dirty-blond forty-nine-year-old CEO of Lighthouse Medical Center. He wears a button-up, a severe frown, and light crow's-feet around the crinkles of his eyes, but I've never seen him crack a smile, so he must do all his laughing off the clock.

He's also Otto's dad and my boss. The fact that I've known him nearly my entire life doesn't mean I get an easy ride—if anything, he's harder on me than anyone. As a new resident fresh out of med school, I have a lot to prove, so I immediately sit up a little straighter in my seat when he addresses me.

"Yes?"

"What're you doing?"

"Nothing." I quickly fold the paper up and stick it in my back pocket.

He's the *last* person who needs the details scrolled on the page.

His eyes flick to my pocket, but he ignores my obvious deceit.

"We're seeing a patient in the east wing. Walk with me."

I'm taller than Dr. Donovan by only a couple of inches, but he's faster, and I have to pick up my pace to keep up as he speed walks to the elevator and punches the button.

It's not uncommon for Dr. Donovan to have me tag along. Since I graduated med school, I've been something of his shadow, following him around while he mentors me on different cases, coaching me through my residency.

I know it's nepotism. I grew up with his son. Our families were tight. When my mother passed in March, he tucked me even tighter under his wing.

But extra attention doesn't mean he's going to make anything easy for me. Even now, waiting on the elevator, I feel a pop quiz coming on.

"How long have you known Mr. Humphrey?" Dr. Donovan asks.

"Mr. Humphrey's Hardware?"

"That's the one."

"All my life."

Hannsett Island is a small tourist town. In the summer, we're packed, but in the off-season, our population dwindles to a couple hundred.

Everyone knows everyone.

The elevator doors open up, and we step inside. Donovan pounds on the Close Door button.

"And how many times have you seen him smile?"

"Once. When Patterson fell off the ladder wrapping wreaths around the lighthouse."

"Exactly. Keep that in mind."

The elevator dings. Donovan exits, his white coat billowing behind him, and I follow him down the hall.

The rooms on the third floor are nice. State-of-the-art equipment, comfortable beds, and full-wall windows. When the curtains are pulled aside, you can look out past the white-and-red striped lighthouse, over the cliff top, and beyond the sparkling blue waters. Miles and miles of crystal blue between Hannsett Island and the mainland, only interrupted by the red-and-green blinking buoys, the joyriders in their sailboats, and the ferry that carries tourists to our small, Margaritaville-style beach town.

It's a good place to sit out the worst days of your life and a reminder that quality of care comes at a price.

At least it did, until Dr. Donovan was instated as the CEO about a decade ago. Half the floor is still sectioned off for people who need anonymity—which often includes celebrities or the rich and famous. The other half is where people go when they're in hospice care or debilitating recovery, regardless of income.

It's how my mother spent her last days looking out over the flat blue coast of Hannsett Island, even though she was a single mom on a bartender's salary.

The point is I owe Dr. Donovan a lot. Which is why I feel even worse holding the secret in my pocket from him.

I follow his lead into room 304. The patient, Hugo Humphrey, is sitting up in the hospital bed. The seventy-one-year-old man is what I'd call "Doc Brown Lite"—he's got a mess of white hair that explodes from either side of his head. His thick eyebrows are constantly furrowed, his mouth forever pinched in a disapproving scowl.

Except for today. Today, he's wearing a wide smile that stretches across his face.

"Look at who we've got here!" Mr. Humphrey exclaims when he sees us. "Diego, boy, don't you look spiffy in your scrubs. Come a long way from stealing candies from my jar, haven't you?"

Then he laughs. It's a strange sound, like a cat coughing up hairballs. I don't think his lungs are used to it.

"Thank you, sir," I say, because I'm not sure how else to respond to that.

This whole thing feels Twilight-Zone-y.

His wife, Helen Humphrey, is a small, slender woman with a gray bowl cut. She keeps her hands in her lap as she sits beside him. Her mouth is fitted with a nervous, pinched smile.

"Someone's in a good mood," Dr. Donovan says. The edges of his eyes crinkle with a smile.

Dr. Donovan might be a grump with his staff, but he's always had good bedside manner with his patients.

"It's nearly Christmas," Mr. Humphrey responds. "What's not to love?"

"You're right about that," Donovan says. "Do you mind if Diego stands in while we talk?"

"Not at all." Mr. Humphrey swings his smiling face between the two of us.

"Great. You wanna tell me what happened?"

"It was the darnedest thing. Helen and I were having breakfast, I got up to fix myself another cup of coffee, and down I went!"

"He fainted," Helen interjects, her voice thin as she fidgets with her hands. "I got him up and immediately took him here."

"Have you been feeling woozy?" Dr. Donovan asks. "Any dizzy spells prior to this?"

Mr. Humphrey shakes his head. "I've been right as rain."

"Mind if I take a look?"

Dr. Donovan plucks his penlight from his pocket. He leans over Mr. Humphrey, and I watch him test the man's pupils. He has Mr. Humphrey follow his finger, then clicks off the light and pockets it.

Dr. Donovan asks if Mr. Humphrey has had any changes in his medication, any other accidents. It's a "no" on both accounts. I take mental notes as I watch them work.

Donovan straightens up once his exam is complete. "Diego will take a blood sample from you, and we'll run some tests. Find out what's going on. You just hang tight and let us know if you need anything in the meantime, alright?"

"Thank you," Helen says. She keeps looking between all three of us, her eyes batting around anxiously.

Something doesn't feel right.

Before we leave, Mr. Humphrey stops us with "Is...Jason here today?"

I can practically see Dr. Donovan's bones stiffen. But he presses on a smile. "I can check. Why do you ask?"

"Hold on—Helen, get my bag." Helen lifts his satchel from the floor and sets it on the bed. Mr. Humphrey starts rummaging through it. He pulls out a book and hands it over.

"If it's not too much trouble," he says, "do you think he could sign it? My daughter-in-law is a big fan. I thought it'd make a good Christmas present for the girl."

It's Dr. King's book, *Cut Out Negativity: Mindfulness & Life Lessons from a Surgeon*. It's got a picture of the doctor on the cover—tall guy with a winning smile.

Dr. Jason King is our own mini celebrity. His book hit the bestsellers list, and he's done the talk show gamut. Honestly? It's pretty cool.

At least, to everyone except Dr. Donovan. He frowns at the book but then takes it and nods. "I'll see what I can do."

"Thanks," Hugo says, still smiling wide.

Donovan and I break out of the patient's room.

"What do you think is wrong with him?" I ask.

Donovan's blue eyes meet mine. "You tell me."

This is a test—one of many he likes to throw at me.

Being a resident underneath Donovan is like learning to drive on the highway. Scary as hell—but you learn fast, and you learn how to do it right.

"Seems like he's got…a bad case of Christmas spirit?"

"Alright. What else? This is your case now."

I think. "A sudden change in behavior could be the result of a brain injury when he fell."

Donovan just listens and nods. "Mmhm."

If he has any better ideas, he doesn't share them.

"So…we should give him a CT scan to make sure," I continue.

"Put it in the system," Dr. Donovan says. "And pull some blood samples."

"Will do."

I start to head down the hall to get the kit, but Donovan turns and adds, "Oh, Diego?"

"Yeah?"

"While you're there, check in on Otto's results, will you?"

Now, my heart does an Olympic-worthy three-point turn in my chest.

Because I've already checked Otto's results. They're sitting in my back pocket.

They're screaming, *High potassium levels. High sodium levels. Toxicity in his blood.*

But Donovan can't know that. Because if he knew, he'd freak out. Then Otto would freak out. And then Otto would never talk to me again.

I'm a terrible liar.

I can't play poker. I can't organize surprise parties.

Everything I feel is always written in big, looping letters on my face.

You have honest eyes, Otto once told me. *It's a good thing.*

I'd blushed—I'm sure he saw that, too.

Fucking honest eyes.

"Okay," I say, trying my best to be stoic. "Will do."

Dr. Donovan, luckily, is in too much of a rush to overthink my painfully panicked response. He just nods and then exits into the elevator.

I exhale a breath as soon as he's out of sight.

The paper in my pocket is practically *burning*.

Liar, liar. Pants on fire.

My phone buzzes, and I reach into my pocket to pull it out. His nose must be itching, because Otto's contact picture (*Otto, standing behind the wheel of his father's boat with big sunglasses, shirt open, a captain's hat, and a goofy smile*) lights up my screen.

[text: Otto] Don't forget, Savage tonight.

I frown at the text. Then I respond:

[text: me] Wouldn't forget.

[text: me] Hey. Just so you know.

[text: me] I've got your results.

[text: me] We have to talk.

Three bubbles pop up. Then nothing. Then three bubbles again, before:

[text: Otto] Later. Let's just enjoy tonight.

I press my lips together. I want to tell him there might not *be* a later if we don't have this conversation.

But that's not something you can say over text. So I just reply:

[text: me] Okay.

I mean to leave it there, but Otto keeps going.

[text: Otto] What are you wearing?

I snap a selfie of my current state—hospital greens.

He sends back:

[text: Otto] Wear that blue button-up you got from Coleman's. It looks good on you.

He adds a couple of "fire" emojis for good measure. I can't help the smile that crosses my lips.

Even when Otto frustrates the hell out of me, he still manages to make me smile.

That, in a nutshell, is why Otto is, has always been, and will always be my kryptonite.

I give his text a thumbs-up react and get back to work, trying to steer clear of thoughts about tonight.

3

NAOMI

I'll never forget my first date with Otto.

We met at his mom's record store. I was browsing through records I'd never buy, and he sidled up to me and asked me if I needed help. I didn't, but I admired his strong arms as he flipped through the albums and gave him my number. We texted back and forth for a couple of days before deciding to meet up. He had a cute smile and could type in full sentences, so I figured, *why not?*

He met me on my turf—Queens, New York City, or as Otto calls it, *the mainland*—and took me out for Mediterranean food at one of the fancier neighborhood hot spots. As he got the check, he said, "By the way. I'm bisexual, polyamorous, and I don't want kids. I'm incredibly into you and love your vibes, but if any of those things are deal breakers for you, let's just be friends."

It'd floored me at first. Not exactly *what* he'd said (we'd unpack each of those items later), but the way he'd said it. I was used to men hiding their truths like razor blades between their teeth. They'd say whatever they needed in order to get into my pants, and only after they were satisfied, they might come out with, *Oh, by the way, I'm married.*

Otto was different. Otto told the whole truth and nothing but the truth.

And damn if that wasn't an aphrodisiac.

I could barely wait to get him back to my place before I had him up against the wall.

I lived (and still live) in a six-story walk-up. I share an apartment with a roommate, a cat, and a whole zoo of critters in my walls that I really try hard not to think about.

Hard to think about anything, really, when I had this beautiful man wedged between my body and the wall. I ravaged his mouth with mine, and he ravaged me right back. His large hands ran down my back until they found the roundness of my ass, and he cupped me there, held me flush against him. I ground my hips into his, and he groaned into my mouth—a deliciously dark, wanting sound that made my skin burn.

My fingers made deft work of his button-up. His shirt hung apart, revealing a slender, hard body underneath.

"Nice scar," I murmured. I traced the raised, pink scar that looked like a crescent moon across his abdomen, vanishing under his belt line.

"I'll tell you all about it."

I nipped his bottom lip. "Later."

I kissed his jaw. His throat. He ravaged me with his hands and his lips, sloppy, hungry kisses. But when I went to unzip his jeans, he suddenly, gently, held my wrists.

"Wait," he said.

I blinked. "Everything okay?"

He nodded. "I just…need a second."

I tilted my head. "First time?"

An amused smile crinkle around his eyes. "No."

"Has it been a while?"

Those intense, blue eyes met mine. "No again."

"Then what's up? 'Cause you're frantic, babe."

"I just feel like I've been waiting for you…for a very long time. And I want to remember this."

When he kissed me again, it was deep. And slow. When his tongue swirled and licked the inside of my mouth, I felt it through every inch of my body. He held me in his arms and kissed me, and kissed me, *and kissed me*, and I felt like I could come from his lips alone.

I *did* come that night. Against the wall. On the floor. In my bed. We fucked like people starving. We fucked until my lips felt swollen and my cunt felt so wonderfully sore and I'd sweat straight through my sheets.

"Jesus Christ." I laughed, swiping my fingers through my damp hair. "What planet are you from?"

He'd just grinned.

Still not entirely sure he isn't alien.

I knew the type of guy Otto was from the first moment we met. He'd *told me*. He was a fuckboy with commitment issues. A privileged white boy who could afford a bohemian artist's lifestyle. A mama's boy who'd always gotten what he wanted and assumed the world would bend to him, not the other way around. And that was *fine*. My plan was simple: I'd ride golden boy's golden cock until I got my share of toe-curling orgasms, and then I'd ghost him when the real thing came along. You know—someone with a three-piece suit and who didn't break out in a sweat at the prospect of so much as swapping keys.

The way I saw it, our relationship had a two-week expiration date, tops.

That was six months ago.

Ever since that first night, Otto and I haven't been able to keep our hands off each other. Otto lives a whopping ferry ride and a trip on the LIRR away from me, but still we make time for each other.

As I got to know him, I began to unpack those truths he'd told me on the first date.

Bisexual. He'd dated both men and women in the past. Didn't discern between the two but tended to lean toward women. Always practiced sex safe, got tested frequently.

Polyamorous. This did not mean a free-for-all sleeping with anyone who showed him the slightest bit of attention. It also didn't mean he was incapable of monogamy. Rather, it meant that, should the right person come along, someone who had that special spark and connection, we'd talk about it, deliberate, and if we were both comfortable with it, there'd be an option there for exploration.

As someone who'd been cheated on consistently in this past, this didn't bother me in the way I thought it would. Instead, when I really took it apart in my brain, I realized it wasn't sharing the other person's body I had a problem with. It was the *lying*. And Otto was nothing if not open.

Lastly, *no kids*. Well, that one was pretty self-explanatory.

I did push him on it, though. Once. His response?

He shrugged, then said, "I'm just not really the kind of guy you want to make long-term plans with."

But he was wrong. Because he's the longest relationship I've ever had, and with each passing day, I'm finding it harder and harder to see my future without him.

And, I think, Otto is getting comfortable with me, too.

I keep waiting for it to slow down. I keep waiting to get bored of him. But neither thing ever comes. Otto is a firecracker, constantly. Every date feels strategically designed to blow the last date out of the water. Every time we have sex, it seems more explosive than the last.

I'm flying high with him, and still, my cynical ass is waiting to hit dirt.

We've had this date on the books for a while. On our third date, he found out my favorite band was an all-female indie punk band called Crystal Savage. They were playing at a Christmas show at an intimate venue called the Banana Peel in December. The tickets were too expensive for me, so

I just mourned the loss and figured I might try scalping tickets at the door the day of. Instead, Otto surprised me at the end of our date with a pair of tickets.

It seemed crazy to me…but not so crazy that I wasn't about to take them. It was July when he gave me the tickets, and I figured if we'd broken up by then (which, with my track record—*yeah*, we probably would), I'd just take one of my girlfriends.

Instead, here we are. Five months later, still going strong, and actually going to the Crystal Savage concert. Together.

The fluttering in my stomach is the stuff of romantic comedies, and I need to pull myself together. Especially because I'm packing some very uh…*intense*…goods between my legs.

After work at Pure Bean Coffee, I have just enough time to book it back to my place and get changed for the concert tonight. It's a Christmas show, so I'm going in all red. Red, tight jeans and a red tank that clings to my curves. Gold hoops in my ears, an explosion of glittering makeup around my eyes, a puffy jacket, and Doc Martens, and we're in business, baby.

The last piece of my outfit is my little early Christmas present Otto got me. The toy is discreet, a pink, U-shaped silicone toy. It's egg-shaped on one end and flat on the other.

I confessed to Otto once that I had a fantasy of being controlled. Otto took my fantasy and ran with it. Because that's the kind of guy he is. No stone left unturned.

And they say gentlemen are a dying breed.

Some women might prefer diamonds. Jewelry. A nice dinner. And, trust me, I like those things, too. But…

I like having *fun* more. And Otto is more than capable of feeding all my kinky desires.

I have a full-length mirror by my bed. I rinse off the toy, take off my pants and panties, and sit on the edge of my bed. I check to make sure it has batteries (it does, praise Otto), and then watch myself in the mirror as I spread my legs. My little bedroom is a mess, but considering it's the size of a closet, it's only fair that it's half bedroom, half closet, half *everything else*. I move the toy between my legs and slip the egg-shaped end against my seam.

I'm already wet. Just the thought of spending the night with this inside of me has me worked up. I bite my lip as the soft egg rubs against my sensitive bits. I gently press it inside of me and gasp when it slides in with zero resistance. The material is soft, comfortable, and even though there's definitely *something* curled inside of me, it's not unpleasant. The U-shaped arm is bendable, and it wraps around, fitting snugly between my lips and resting against my clit.

I already feel my body buzzing with excitement at the sight of it. I take out my phone, spread my legs, and snap a picture of myself in the mirror. I send it to Otto with the text:

[text: me] Ready for tonight.

He responds only seconds later:

[text: Otto] Jesus.

[text: Otto] You're so bloody hot.

[text: Otto] I nearly fell out of my chair.

I can't help but grin. A worked-up Otto is my favorite type of Otto.

[text: me] Wanna test it out?

[text: Otto] Later. I'm writing.

Otto's writing time is sacred. He writes slice-of-life stories, quasi-autobiographical pieces about living in Long Island, being an outcast, feeling strange in your own skin. He got a kidney transplant at the age of twelve. Plus, he grew up with two dads and a mom, who all live together in a polyamorous triad. So he has a lot of material to work with. His short stories have been published in literary magazines across the state, and I'm proud of him.

But I'm also needy.

[text: me]
[text: Otto] Be good.

But I'm not good at *being good*. Especially when I'm already pulsing around the toy, and I want so badly for Otto to flip it on and bring me to a quick, explosive climax.

So I snap another picture—this time, I'm flipping him the bird.

In response, Otto sends me a selfie of himself mid–eye roll.

I can't help but cackle a laugh.

Otto is a guy who likes nice things. He likes dressing up, combing back his hair, buzzing out the perfect soft shadow of stubble around his jaw, and adding a touch of cologne. He knows the best angles for a group photo and how to wear a million-dollar smile.

But here's a secret I'll never tell him: I like him most like he is in the selfie he sent just now. Untamed hair, tired eyes, glasses on, semi-slouched in his chair. He's such a picture-perfect guy that I find him most attractive when he's just a little bit messy.

So I send back:

[text: me] Fiiiine.
[text: me] Can't wait to see you tonight.
[text: Otto] Can't wait.

I shoot him a kissy-face emoji for good measure. Then I shimmy my clothes back on and adjust the toy a bit inside my pants to make sure there's no awkward bulge. It stays put surprisingly well, and by the time I finish getting ready and make my way onto the subway, I've almost forgotten it's there.

There's one errand I want to run before showtime.

K-Records is a record store on St. Mark's Place, an alternative, hip street in downtown Manhattan. I used to come here to trade in my shoes at the used clothes store, which always had leftovers from the old, crusty punk generation.

While the street still retains its old favor, it's grown up over the years and is now pocketed with upscale boutiques and yoga studios.

But K-Records is its only little blast from the past. It's a basement-level store, and I descend the steps to the entrance, where immediately I'm blasted with a hard-rock '90s band wailing on the stereos.

"Miss Kenzi?" I call out.

The record store has crates and crates of records on display. Vintage finds on the back wall. New releases near the door. Bowls of pins. Novelty T-shirts. They have K-Records shirts (I own one myself) on display: black shirts with the mascot, a hip muskrat DJ spinning records. No idea how Kenzi picked *muskrat*, but it's a cute logo.

I go to the desk, a glass case with bits and pieces of local jewelry on display underneath, and lean over it to try to find the owner. "Hello? Anyone here?"

"Hi!" Kenzi peeks her head out of a door in the back and calls out over the music, "Be right there!"

She closes the door, and I rest my elbows on the counter and wait. I'm only waiting a couple of minutes before Kenzi re-enters, looking a little disheveled but smiling widely.

"Good to see you, Naomi. Sorry, I was doing a bit of organization in the back. Let me turn this down—jeez, I didn't realize how high I'd cranked it."

"I like it," I tell her.

Kenzi is the kind of woman I want to be when I'm her age. Curvy, confident, with long dark hair that she's dyed blue at the tips. She owns the record store, which is how I got to know her initially.

Falling for her son was just the cherry on top of an already sweet cake.

She picks up a remote and turns the music down just a bit so we can actually hear each other speak. "Aren't you supposed to be at the concert tonight?"

"Yep. I just wanted to grab something first. Are you still holding *Doolittle*?"

A smile climbs Kenzi's face. "Is it time?"

I shrug. "Tonight just feels special."

She's been holding the Pixies' album *Doolittle* for me for almost a month now. It's $40, which is big change when you're a tattoo artist who spends most of her money going back and forth to Long Island to visit her practically long-distance boyfriend. But the Pixies are Otto's favorite band, and he gives me *so much...*

I just want to give him a little something in return.

"Jason!" Kenzi shouts over her shoulder. The back door cracks open, and a man sticks his head out.

"Yep?"

"The Pixies. *Doolittle*. Third shelf on the left."

"Copy that."

The door closes, and seconds later, Jason comes out with my record in hand. He steps behind the counter, slots himself behind Kenzi, and sets my record on the counter.

"Hey, Naomi. How goes it?"

"Good, Mr. King."

He scrunches his nose. "That's my dad. Just Jason."

"Sorry, Mr....Jason."

It's been drilled into my head to be polite to your partners' parents, and it's a hard habit to kick. Jason is Otto's dad —well, *one* of Otto's dads. Otto has two fathers, technically: Jason and Donovan. Jason, Donovan, and Kenzi have been together for years. When Otto told me the first time, it blew my mind. Now? I kinda love it.

It also helped explain his aversion to the one-partner idea. His parents make the poly thing look so appealing.

And by appealing, I mean...*appealing*.

Jason is well over six feet, with raven-black hair, a linebacker's body, and the same piercingly blue eyes that Otto has.

Is it wrong to thirst over your boyfriend's hot dad?

Ugh.

Unfortunately (or fortunately, depending on how you look at it), Jason is one of the good ones. He does that thing that good guys do when a hot twenty-four-year-old saunters into their personal space wearing combat boots and a *ready to fuck in the alleyway* attitude. He holds his wife a little tighter and nuzzles into the crook of her neck.

Again. *A good guy.*

"How's the…um…organizing going?" Kenzi asks.

"Super organized," Jason replies, arm hooked around Kenzi's middle, and presses a kiss to her neck.

Kenzi blushes, and it's obvious that they've been doing everything *except* organizing the closet.

I snort a laugh. I want to tell them they don't have to hide from me; it's refreshing. My parents barely held hands in front of their kids. It's nice to see people who can't keep their hands off each other, even after years together.

Otto spent most of his life without a father. He didn't meet Jason until he was already twelve. Yet somehow, the two have a lot in common. A chiseled jawline. That boyish, lopsided smile. And, apparently, a hell of a sex drive.

Like father, like son.

Kenzi rings me up with a "That'll be $20."

I blink. "Is it on sale?"

She just gives me a knowing smile. "Friends-and-family discount."

"You really don't have to—*oh.*"

But my sweet, heart-warming moment with Otto's mom is cut short.

Because suddenly, I start *vibrating*.

The toy between my legs buzzes. It's quiet, but I can feel it, a rapid hum massaging my inner walls. Nestled between my folds, the arm buzzes *directly* against my sensitive nub.

The pleasure is so intense that, for a second, my breath catches in my throat and gets stuck there.

It's a shock, and I stumble forward. Jason's reflexes are quick, and he reaches across the counter to grab my shoulder, holding me upright.

"Hey," he says, those blue eyes flickering between my own, examining me. "Are you okay?"

When he's not screwing his wife in the back room, he's a surgeon at Hannsett Island. Their top surgeon, actually. So I recognize that he's trying to be helpful, trying to make sure I'm not about to faint in their shop.

But I don't want him to see my dilated pupils or my flushed cheeks or the way my thighs have to squeeze together.

I bite the inside of my lip to keep from moaning out loud and pull myself together. "Yeah—no. It's fine. I'm fine. Just a...weird spell is all...*ah!*"

If that wasn't enough...the vibrations get *more* intense. Every nerve inside of me lights up as bolts of pleasure rocket through my blood. I gasp and find myself clinging to Jason's arm, digging my nails in, *trying* not to scream.

His eyebrows lift. "Naomi. Are you sure you're okay?"

Kenzi looks concerned, too. Quickly, I'm brought back to earth.

I'm in a record store. In public. *In front of my boyfriend's parents.*

I want nothing more than to grab this desk, squeeze my thighs together, and hump my way through a blinding orgasm against the merciless vibrations of the toy, but I'm *not* about to do that here.

So I smile weakly instead and stammer through an explanation. "Something I ate...sorry...$1 pizza...don't trust it. Thanks for the record! Have a good one!"

I release Otto's dad from my death grip, slam a twenty down on the counter, grab the record, and rush through goodbyes before racing out of the shop. It's dirty New York City air out here, but I gulp it in anyway and feel grateful for the icy winter temperature that immediately chills my skin.

It's not a cold shower, but it helps.

Finally, the toy stops its onslaught. I catch my breath—or try to, anyway.

I get shocked with another vibration. But this one isn't coming between my legs.

It's in my pocket. I pull out my phone and see Otto's name across the screen.

I pick up.

"Hey, babe," Otto says, cool as a cucumber. His voice is crisp, masculine, and has a hint of an accent. He spent the first decade of his life in England, and though he's mostly adapted an American dialect, every now and then, his *r's* go rhotic or his *h's* go quiet.

So it's more of an *Ey* than a *Hey*. Something I'd normally think is endearing.

Right now, I just think he's an ass.

I roll my eyes. "Hey, dick."

I can practically *hear* his smugness in his voice. "Does it work?"

"Sure does," I tell him. "I nearly came in your dad's arms. So. Thank you for that."

A *looooong* silence on the other end.

"Uhh. What? Which dad?"

I snort a laugh. "Your first response is *which dad*? Does it make a difference?"

"Kinda."

"Jason. I was at your mom's shop."

"Ah. Makes sense."

Otto and Jason have a strange, always loving but sometimes strained relationship. Otto never talks about it, but it's always there, like oil shimmering on the surface of a still lake.

I sigh. "Maybe a little warning next time?"

"Warning," Otto says.

"Huh?"

The buzz shoots through me.

"*Fuck.*" I swear between my teeth. My knees buckle. My hardened nipples chafe against my shirt. Just when I've gotten myself under control, I immediately rocket to the edge of pleasure again.

"Sorry. Was that mean?"

"Very."

"Hmm. Maybe I'm feeling a little mean."

"Are you punishing me?"

"No." *Buzz.* "Well." *Buzz.* "Maybe a little." *Buzz.*

My breath catches in my throat. I stumble on the sidewalk, and I have to brace myself against a bus stop pole. The vibrations are relentless, and they whisper through my body, hitting deep inside of me and nestling against my swollen nub.

It's thirty degrees and I'm sweating in my overcoat.

"You're going to make me come," I whisper.

"No. I'm not." And suddenly, the vibrations cease. "Not until tonight, anyway. You have to wait on that."

My thighs are shaking. I'm throbbing, and my body wants *so badly* to reach that pleasurable peak, but the torment is delicious.

"Otto?"

"Yeah?"

I bite my lip. "Stay mad."

"Why?"

"I want you to pound me at the back of the club tonight."

A low groan leaves Otto's throat, and it sends a rippling thrill through me.

If I have to suffer until tonight, he does, too.

"You're in so much trouble," he says.

I grin. "Promises, promises…"

4

OTTO

The Banana Peel is a music venue located where a warehouse once was. Like most things in New York, the cover doesn't tell the full story. It looks like a simple brick-and-tin building on the outside, but on the inside, it has three full bars, a wraparound balcony, and a dance floor in the center flanked by roped-off VIP tables.

Every year, they have a holiday rock show called the "12 Nights of Rockmas." For twelve days, they have sold-out shows, each night featuring a different band. They do a mix of rebooted Christmas music, as well as their more popular songs.

The festival is a hit every season. The tickets aren't cheap, especially not for a band as popular as Crystal Savage, but I believe if there's anything worth spending money on, it's travel, music, and food. In that order.

Which is why I bought the three of us a VIP table for the experience.

Well. Which is why I *mostly bought* the tickets.

Diego helped. As he always does when I splurge. But that's the cost of having a writer for a roommate—my money situation isn't always stable. I'm lucky to have a friend like Diego, who doesn't mind putting in.

I call him my sugar roomie. He claims he doesn't like the title, but it always makes him laugh.

Diego and I dust off the snow and sit on the iron steps, waiting for Naomi to show. I'm wearing a black button-up, slim pants, a leather wristband, and a couple of bulky rings on my fingers. Going for the *rocker's night out* look. Diego is tucked into a cozy sweater with Christmas trees knitted into it and his blue button-up underneath. He keeps glancing at the time on his phone.

"The opening band is already on," he complains.

"Relax," I tell him, planting my hands on the icy steps behind me. "Openers always suck."

The corner of his mouth dips into a frown. "Says the man who gets mad when we miss the trailers."

"That's because *trailers* are usually better than the actual movies. Openers are like…warm-up."

"Cold."

I take a handful of snow from the pile behind me and toss it at him. White powder trickles into the neck of his sweater, and he finally cracks a smile.

When we were kids, I used to be the worrywart. I'd worry when my mom left my sight. I'd worry when we were running late. I'd worry about what was in my food. I'd worry about gray clouds and pending rain. After spending years in and out of hospitals with no diagnosis in sight, my worries seemed legitimate.

Then, when I was twelve, life changed. Dramatically. Mom and I moved from London to Hannsett Island, a seaside town in Long Island where she'd spent a summer in her youth. I met Jason, who turned out to be my biological father. I also met Adam Donovan, and though we weren't genetically related, we connected on a different level. My condition had gone unchecked for too long, and I needed a new kidney. Donovan gave me his. We've been attached ever since—I carry a piece of him around inside of me. *He's* keeping me alive.

That's something I don't forget. Not ever.

When I got my new kidney, it was like the world opened up. I climbed out of the shadows and into the sunshine. I wanted to experience life, all of it—the good, the bad, and the ugly. When I was old enough to date, I dated everyone. Boys, girls, whatever. It didn't matter. I said *fuck fear* and took my short stories out of the drawer and started submitting them to prestigious literary magazines—and even got into a few of them. I did the polar bear plunge in the winter. I tried lollipops with scorpions embedded in the candy. I got a driver's license, and a motorcycle license, and a motorboat license. I did it all.

Naomi came at the right time. She was the only person I'd ever met who had the same wild, chaotic energy as I did. She leapt before she looked, and I found that unbearably attractive.

Diego, on the other hand, started out as my wild and reckless playmate and, as he grew up, became more reserved. Quieter. When his mother lost her battle with cancer earlier this year, he stopped talking completely. It was a stark, eerie contrast from the boy who could rattle off theories about Marvel movies for an hour without stopping to take a breath. There were some nights we'd go out to the beach, and we'd just sit there in silence, listening to the water break on the shore.

He's crawled out of his shell bit by bit since, but it's like there are ropes around his ankles now. There's always something holding him back. I always get the feeling he's biting his tongue.

Like now, when he stares at me, and I can feel there's something heavy weighing on his mind.

"Penny for your thoughts?" I pry.

He looks reluctant to say anything. I can tell he's weighing his words, contemplating. Finally, he comes out with "We have to talk about your blood results at some point. Soon."

His words are heavy as lead inside of me. With my condition, I have to go to Lighthouse Medical once a month to get a round of blood tests and make sure everything is copesetic. Because I'm the CEO's son, I get perks. Mainly, I get to pick my doctor, which is why Diego pulls my blood and takes my results every time.

The last couple of months, the levels of toxicity in my blood have been rising. Fast. It's not uncommon. It's been eighteen years, after all. Well past the life expectancy of my organ. Now, all signs point to oncoming kidney failure. I should know. I've been here before. The hot sweats. The dizzy spells. The dull ache in my back. Restless, uncomfortable nights.

I begged Diego to keep quiet about it, because I knew my dads would freak out. He promised he would. But I can tell from the look in his eyes, it's weighing on him.

I'd love to comfort him. Tell him everything will be okay. But I can't.

Because the truth is…the thing I haven't told *anyone*, not even Diego…

I'm not getting another transplant.

Donovan gave this kidney to me. He *trusted* me with it. And I'll be damned if I give it up. Even if it kills me.

"Later," I say. "We'll talk about it later. Let's just enjoy tonight."

Diego doesn't look thrilled by that answer, but he nods and stares across the street, honoring my request.

"Here she comes," he says—and thank god, I've been saved by the bell.

Or the *belle*. Naomi is a bombshell. Skintight red jeans and a crimson shirt underneath a faux-fur-lined parka. Her long, dark hair flows over her shoulders, and those devious brown eyes sparkle.

Best of all, I know what she's wearing *underneath* all that. The little vibrator snuggled up inside of her.

And suddenly, I'm not thinking about my kidney. Or Diego's increasing concern.

All I can think about is getting her someplace dark and private and slotting my face between her thighs.

I kick off from the steps and meet her at the end of the block, scooping her up in my arms. Her parka is so puffy, it's like hugging a marshmallow, and half of her deflates in my arms.

"Hey, you." She grins, and my heart does backflips.

"Hey."

I kiss her. It's freezing cold out here, but the inside of her mouth is hot, and I'm hungry for it. My worries and anxieties melt away under the heat of her kiss.

One more night, I think to myself.

One more perfect, beautiful night with the perfect woman and your best friend. Savor this now. Savor this while you can.

I kiss her like it's the last time my lips will ever touch hers, and the both of us are breathless when we part. I can see her breath frosting in the air, white puffs.

"Should we...um. Inside?" she asks.

"My thoughts exactly."

5

NAOMI

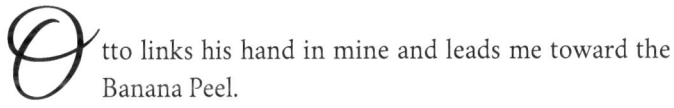

*O*tto links his hand in mine and leads me toward the Banana Peel.

Even the small touch of his fingers sends small tingles of excitement through me. One kiss from him and I'm already reeling.

I can't shake the feeling. *Tonight is special.*

I don't know how or why, exactly; there's just a different energy around tonight. It's got me on pins and needles in a good way.

I live for the thrill, after all, and Otto is nothing if not thrill incarnate.

We approach the building, and a familiar figure gets to his feet. Diego looks fresh, cleanly shaved in a nice, fitting sweater. My heart warms when I see him. "Diego!" I shout. "I didn't know you'd be here!"

"Oh," Otto says, realization suddenly dawning. "Yeah. I invited him. I forgot to tell you. Sorry."

By which he means *sorry I forgot to tell you*, not *sorry he's here*.

Diego's eyes widen at that. He looks at Otto, then at me, then back to Otto again. "Is it okay?"

"Of course," I laugh and wrap my arms around him. "It's good to see you, buddy."

"You too."

I'm surprised but also not surprised. Wherever Otto goes, Diego is his shadow and vice versa.

I met Diego on my second date with Otto. Looking back on it, it's a miracle Diego didn't show up to my *first* date with Otto. For as long as I've known them, the two men have been joined at the hip. They shared childhood memories. Inside secrets. They had an entire language of eye contact and raised eyebrows that I could only try to decipher.

I'll admit, I was afraid Diego and I wouldn't hit it off. I didn't know what to make of the clean-shaven, handsome Brazilian man at first. He was quiet, reserved, and what I like to call an *angel boy*. He buttoned his shirt up to the top button. He carried a bottle of water wherever he went. He didn't do drugs—not even weed—and I caught the distinct, judgmental downturn of his lips when I offered him a toke from my one-hitter.

So, yeah. For a while there, Diego and I went together like peanut butter and queso.

But eventually, somewhere in the silent spaces when Otto left us alone, we got to talking. It turns out, we have more in common than we have dissimilar. We're both horror-movie fanatics (James Wan is a genius, and no one can convince me otherwise). We both come from immigrant parents and know full well the complications that can come along with that. We both agree that breakfast is the most important meal of the day, and brunches are *mandatory* on Saturdays. And, most importantly, we both love Otto.

But the thing we bonded over—and I mean, *really* bonded over—was when we showed up at Otto's family Thanksgiving table in November. Otto is lucky. He has a big, loving family—one mom, two dads. It's an unconventional relationship, but the three of them have been together since Otto was twelve. Donovan, CEO at Lighthouse Medical. Jason, surgeon and TV personality. And Kenzi, record store owner and life of the party. The oddest part is how *not strange* it is. They did all the "normal" family things—Donovan snapped at Jason when he nearly burned the stuffing. Kenzi told Otto's kidney-transplant story and called him "the bravest boy," which made Otto turn red. Jason added songs that no one wanted to the Thanksgiving playlist, which caused a row.

But it was their quiet moments of intimacy that really punched me in the chest. I was helping clear the table, Jason stationed at the sink, and I caught something I wasn't supposed to see: Donovan slipping behind Jason, murmuring an *I'm sorry* into his ear and then softly kissing the back of the other man's neck. Jason just smiled. When Donovan saw me watching them, he'd pulled away, thanked me for carrying in the dishes, and then went to where Kenzi was sitting on the couch and laid his head down in her lap.

It hit me suddenly, out of nowhere—this pain in my chest that knocked all the air out of my lungs. I excused myself and slipped outside the sliding glass doors to the patio.

Their family house sat right on the beach. It was a dark night, the moon hiding behind thick clouds, and I could barely make out the black sea, but I could hear it softly lapping at the shore. I took out a cigarette, lit it up, and watched the ember burn in the dark.

I hadn't thought this plan all the way through, and I was freezing in my camisole. But I needed the silence more than I needed warmth, so I toughed it out.

The sliding door opened and shut behind me. "Hey. I thought you might want this."

Diego had come out to check in on me. Of course he did. *Angel boy.*

He was holding my leather jacket. I took it and slipped it on. "Thanks."

35

He stood beside me, and for a minute, we just lingered in the dark. The warm lights from the house backlit his face, and I could see him leaning on the railing with me, watching the outline of the ocean.

"Are you okay?" he asked finally.

"Yeah. Holidays can just…get a little hard."

I felt him staring at me.

"Who'd you lose?" he asked.

I rolled up my long sleeve to show him the date I have tattooed on my wrist. "My dad. Lost him five years ago."

He nodded sympathetically. Then he unbuttoned his shirt —that top button, down his chest. He peeled his collar back to show me the angel tattoo printed on his shoulder. "My mother," he replied. "March. Cancer."

After that, we were thick as thieves.

I love Otto. I love him to the moon and back. I love him in ways I never thought I would ever love anyone. But losing my father was the hardest pain I ever had to go through. That's something Otto—who has not one, but *two* living fathers—can't understand.

Diego gets it, though. It's something we share, a bond of grief that goes deep.

So it's *genuinely* good to see him tonight. The night wouldn't feel right without him.

I release Diego from my hug and hook one arm in Diego's, the other in Otto's. "Alright, guys and geeks," I tell them. "You ready to rock the fuck out?"

Otto lets out an affirmative whooping sound, and Diego just grins.

We join the long line of people shivering while they wait to go inside. Otto flashes his tickets from his phone, and the bouncer stamps the backs of our hands. It's a monkey in a Santa hat inked on the back of my hand, and it makes me smile.

"Next tattoo?" I ask Otto, showing him the stamp.

"Definitely," he says.

I'm feeling goofy and light.

The second we go inside, we're met with a toe-tingling heat. It's the warmth of bodies pressed up together, moving like a wave on the dance floor. I've only been to this venue a couple of times before, and I marvel now at the color lights that flicker across the intimate space, illuminating the crowd below.

They've decked it out for the holidays. Giant, multicolored Christmas balls hang from the ceiling. The walls are strung up with wreaths and twinkle lights. Everyone is wearing something festive—Santa hats, ugly sweaters, and I even spot someone with a Menorah ornamenting the top of their head.

The opening band is wrapping up now, and they're blaring their final song. I can barely hear Otto as he steers both Diego and me through the crowd. We move to the back, which is blocked off with red velvet rope and a frightening-looking bouncer. He checks Otto's tickets once more and then grants us access.

It's a little calmer back here. There are a few tables and booths, and the bouncer lifts the "reserved" sign off one of the red semicircle booths. The first thing I do is shimmy out of my jacket, and the three of us make a pile of winter clothes on the far side of the booth.

I scoot in beside Otto. A waiter with a red Rudolph nose comes over, and he can't hear Diego, so I yell out our drink orders for all three of us. Jack and Coke for me, IPA for Diego, and seltzer water for Otto.

"This," I say, leaning back against the booth, "is too cool. These tickets must've been insane."

Otto shrugs. "Worth it."

Knowing Otto too well, I lean across him to look at Diego and say, "Thanks, sugar roomie."

That gets a little smile from Diego. "My pleasure. Really."

Otto winds his arm around my back. I feel him grip my hip, and his thumb slowly rubs and up down my side. "Having fun?"

"Yes."

"Good. Because the night hasn't even gotten started."

With that, Otto pulls out his phone and starts flipping through it. I know what's coming next, and the anticipation makes me dig my heels against the floor. He starts me off slow, a low humming, like butterfly wings beating against my cunt. I'm so sensitive that even the light tickle of the vibrator forces me to bite the inside of my lip to keep from moaning.

"Did you have to work today?" Otto asks Diego. Casual as anything.

"Yeah," Diego says.

"Anything fun?"

Diego starts to recount a story—something about a guy with what he calls "a bad case of too much Christmas." But I'm having a hard time concentrating. Our drinks come, and I wrap my hands tightly around the glass. I try to focus on anything else—the coldness of the glass, the pounding of the music, the soothing timber of Diego's voice as he talks. But my body has other ideas. I find myself squirming in my seat, half grinding against the toy. If I push my ass back in the seat, I can rock forward with small, imperceptible movements and grind my aching clit against the teasing toy.

Otto can feel my movements, though. I can tell because he gives my hip a small squeeze, encouraging.

"Hey," Otto says, and his voice breaks me out of a particularly good rut. I'm short of breath, and I blink upward to see that he's lifted his glass, "to my favorite people."

I hold up my drink as well. "And a great fucking night," I add.

"I'll drink to that," Diego says.

We clink glasses and take a sip. I've only just swallowed

when the toy suddenly ramps up. It feels like a hand stroking my inner walls and rubbing my sensitive nub.

I yelp without meaning to. Otto snickers and cuts the vibrations completely.

Now, I'm just panting, my heart pounding, and Otto looks far too pleased with himself.

Diego glances between us. "Am I missing something?"

Otto turns to me. "Can I tell him?"

I blush. It's embarrassing…but not for the right reasons.

I'm embarrassed to confess the truth…I *want* Otto to tell Diego. I want him to know. I want *everyone* to know that Otto has my pleasure completely and utterly locked under his control. I want them to know that he can bring me to dizzying heights with a single swipe of his finger.

I want everyone to know that I'm Otto's good girl. Otto's perverse little slut.

The thought is so erotic that, even though my little friend is dormant for now, my pussy throbs around it.

I nod, giving Otto my consent. He puts his phone on the table in front of Diego and says, "Watch this."

He touches the screen and draws his finger slowly upward. I gasp and clutch at the seat as the vibrator jumps to life. As he traces his fingertip upward, the vibrations grow more and more intense. My thighs clench together, my hips push forward, and my head drops back as I'm unable to hold back a moan.

"She's wearing a vibrator," Otto explains. "It's wirelessly connected to this app. I can turn it on, turn it off, increase the vibrations—it's even got rhythms. Check this out."

He presses a couple of buttons, and suddenly, the vibrator starts *pulsing*. I gasp and lean forward, gripping the table so tightly, my knuckles go white. The pulses are intense, and they rub against a sweet spot inside of me that makes my body go tight.

"Otto…" I whimper in warning. I'm getting close. *Really* close.

He cuts the toy, and I gulp in a breath I didn't realize I was holding. But my body is still buzzing, and I wiggle in my seat, finding it hard to come down from the edge.

"Jesus," Diego says, and his voice has gotten deeper, a little hoarse. "You're like an evil Steve Hawkins."

Otto laughs at that. He slips his hand to the back of my neck and gives me a squeeze. I lean into his grip, needing his touch, melting into his hands.

"Poor thing," Otto says, but his tone is mocking, merciless. "I've had her worked up all day. Every time I flick it on, she's like, seconds away from busting."

I shiver in his touch.

What is wrong with me that it turns me on when they talk about me like this?

Why does that darkly mischievous look in Otto's eyes make me flood my panties?

The truth is—I've dated mean guys before. Been fucked over by them.

Otto isn't a mean guy. Otto is a *good guy*. He just likes playing mean, because it turns the both of us on.

And at the end of the day, it's not the vibrator, or the degradation, or the role-play that arouses me. It's the *trust*. Every time he looks at me or touches me, I know his eyes are asking—*is this okay?*

And every time I bite my lip or meet his gaze, I'm replying—*yes, please. More, please*.

We know each other so well at this point, sometimes, that's all it takes.

Over the roar of the music, Otto shifts to press his body against mine. I lean into the strong warmth of him. He tilts toward me, and I can feel his breath on my ear.

"I want to give Diego my phone, and I want to take you

dancing," Otto says, loud enough so I can hear it, but only me. "What do you think?"

The thought sends a shiver through me. I didn't think it was possible, but I can feel myself getting even wetter in response.

I bite my lip. "Yes. Okay."

He takes my chin, forces my head upward toward his, and kisses me. It's a slow, possessive kiss. It says, *Don't forget who you belong to*.

I don't. I never could.

Otto leans over and murmurs to Diego. Diego's eyes go wide, glance at me, and then he nods. Otto pushes his phone across the table, takes my hand, and drags me out of the VIP lounge and into the throng of bodies. I glance over my shoulder and see Diego with his head down, already tapping away at Otto's phone. Inspecting the app, no doubt.

Diego is a bit of a technology whiz, so it's very possible that this is dangerous in his hands. The thought makes me shiver.

Otto draws me against his body and holds me. The opening act came and went, and now Crystal Savage is on. His hands slide down the small of my back, and as I sway against him, I start to feel the vibrations pick up between my legs.

I moan. My cunt is wound tight. Diego is, as I expected, having too much fun. Vibrations turn into pulses and then into waves of unending pleasure.

I can barely stand upright. I fall against Otto and envelop myself in him. His crisp, smoky cologne. His strong, powerful arms.

The music surrounds me like a hug. I feel like I'm high—falling, tripping into sounds and sensations.

"I love this song," I whimper into Otto's shirt.

"I love this song, too," he murmurs into my ear.

His voice is heady and deep, and I can hear his smile.

It's like he's not talking about the song.

It feels like he's talking about *me*.

And maybe that's what does it—the pulse of the music, the intensity of the toy, and the warm affection in Otto's voice.

I hit my crescendo.

I shout and cling to Otto. I can't keep my composure anymore—I fall apart on the dance floor. He holds me, kissing my throat, my face, as I throb and pulse, the toy pulling my pleasure from me over and over again.

The song ends, and the crowd goes wild. It feels like they're cheering for me.

"Good girl," Otto murmurs. "Give me everything."

I whimper and shiver and ride out my orgasm, swaying in his arms.

6

DIEGO

*O*tto and Naomi escape to the dance floor, and I'm having too much fun.

The app on Otto's phone is, on its face, pretty simple. It's designed like a graph with a small dot in the center. You can drag the dot up and down the graph, increasing or decreasing the intensity of the toy.

But I click around. I find loops. Programs designed for different sensations—short bursts, slow builds, and patterns of varying intensity.

I play with them all, knowing that Naomi is experiencing it in real time.

I've never done anything like this before. It should be strange, making my best friend's girlfriend tremble from across the room.

But, somehow? This feels easy. Natural.

I look across the room. I can't see Naomi's face—she's buried it in Otto's chest. He's holding her, whispering in her ear.

As if he can feel my stare, his eyes lift and catch mine.

There's a heat in his gaze that makes me burn.

I turn the program up. All the way up.

Naomi's knees buckle, and she fists his shirt.

His eyes don't leave mine, though. He holds her, murmurs in her ear, and smirks. Then he *winks* at me.

As if to say, *Good job.*

I swallow. Hard.

I've gotten carried away. I'm stiff and pinned awkwardly against my thigh, and I have to reach under the table and have to adjust myself through my pants.

Just then, the waiter comes by with a second round of drinks.

He startles me, and I quickly retract my hand from my lap. Too quickly.

My elbow bumps into my glass, and my beer upends, spilling out across the table, foamy and thick.

"Oh *shit*!" I say.

"Sorry," the waiter says, doing his best to mop it up. "I'll get you another."

But it's not the beer I'm worried about.

I grab a napkin and quickly dab Otto's phone clean. That little dot is still at the top of the screen, all the way up, holding Naomi at its highest intensity.

I stab at the screen with my finger, but…nothing. I try the buttons on the side.

The app doesn't respond. The phone won't turn off.

It doesn't stop going.

The waiter leaves, and Otto and Naomi return to the table.

Naomi is, understandably, a mess.

"Please," she mewls against Otto, still clinging to him little a kitten. "Please, please, *please*!"

Otto flashes a grin at me. "Hey, man. Cut it."

"I can't." I hold up his phone guiltily to show the damage. "It's stuck."

Otto's eyebrows rocket up his forehead. Then he lets out a laugh. "Okay, baby girl. You're in trouble."

"*Please!*" she begs, and she sounds legitimately strained. "I can't, fuck, I can't take any more—"

"Lay down." Naomi settles into the booth, getting on her back. Otto glances around and tells me, "Cover us."

I don't know what that means. Literally. I don't know how to cover two people when one is squirming like all hell and the other has his hand between her thighs. I could drape a jacket over them, but I'm pretty sure that would draw attention toward us, not away from us. But I glance around the bar and try to make sure no one's coming after us.

I'm also trying to keep my gaze averted from what's happening *right next to me.*

There's the hiss of Naomi's zipper. I hear Naomi gasp, and I know Otto's fingers are inside of her.

"Good girl," he murmurs. "You're doing so good."

Then I hear the buzzing. He pulls the toy out and dangles it. It's U-shaped and glistening.

Naomi has her hand over her face. She might be crying.

"I'm sorry," I blurt out, shame running through me like cold water. "I'm so sorry. Are you okay?"

But then she starts to *laugh.*

It's loud and long. A huge, cackling laugh with pitches and squeaks and gasps for breath.

"Oh. My. *God*," she says when she can finally speak. "I think I came like twenty times."

Otto, too, is grinning at me.

"You broke my phone," he says. "And my girlfriend."

"Sorry," I say for what feels like the thirtieth time.

Naomi is still sprawled out on the seat, Otto positioned on top of her. He moves his thumb to the bottom of the pink toy, I assume to a button there, and it stops vibrating.

"How're you feeling?" he asks Naomi.

"Fucking fantastic."

Then Otto covers her toy in his hand. His eyes locked on hers, he swirls his tongue around the bulb of it.

Unbidden, the thought pops into my mind: *I wonder what that tongue would feel like if—*

No. Let's not go there.

Naomi laughs. "Animal."

He grins. "Slut."

She grips his shirt and yanks him against her. They kiss, deeply, and I have to look away.

I wish there was a way to discreetly move my beer to my lap so the cold glass could help relieve the parts of me that have suddenly become unbearably swollen.

I wish the sight of the two of them didn't take the breath out of my lungs.

I wish the three of us—

Stop. Let's not *wish* too close to the sun.

Eventually, the two of them break apart. Even with my gaze at the band, I can feel Otto's eyes on me.

"Come on," he says. "Let's dance. All of us."

7

NAOMI

*T*he rest of the night goes by in a blur.

We dance. We drink. I'm on cloud nine.

No, cloud *ten.* I'm on clouds that didn't exist before tonight.

We dance our hearts out, and Crystal Savage kills it. The show ends, and the three of us spill out from the oppressive heat into the chilled city night.

It feels good. Refreshing.

Diego peels away from us and starts to head toward the glowing orb lantern above the train station.

"Diego!" I call out, and he turns, one foot already descending the staircase. "Why don't you come over for a bit?"

He glances at the clock on his phone. "The LIRR shuts down in an hour."

"So you have an hour." I lean against Otto. I savor the heat of him. The hardness of his body. He winds his arms around my middle, keeping me close.

"Come on," Otto urges. "It'll be fun."

Diego hesitates still. Then, he climbs back up the steps and shoves his hands in his pockets, heading back to us.

"One drink," he says.

* * *

The three of us pile into my shoebox apartment. I call out my roommate's name, but no one responds.

"Just us," I announce. I hang my jacket, and the other two follow suit. "Sit where you want."

There's not a lot of options—the beat-up sofa or the worn-in lounge chair I found on Craigslist. Otto snags the chair, and Diego takes the couch.

"Tea?" I ask.

"Oh, yes," Otto says. "Please."

"Sure," Diego replies.

I have to scoop Milo, the tabby cat, off the stove before I put the kettle on. I didn't use to be a tea girl, but Otto turned me on to that, too.

Milo yowls angrily when I remove him from his spot and trots over to the living room. There's no real divider between the kitchen and the living room, so I watch as Milo inspects the boys, tail swishing. Otto leans over and extends a hand, *pst-pst-pst*ing.

Milo leaps on the couch and climbs into Diego's lap instead. Diego pets Milo, and the cat's tail crooks upward.

"Traitor," Otto complains.

While the kettle is going, I sneak into my bedroom. My bag from the record shop rests against my drawer. I pull out *Doolittle*, take it from the sleeve, and carry it back into the living room.

Technically, the focal point of the living room is the TV. My roommate and I veg out here more times than I can count. My dad's old record player sat completely unused for months in the corner of the room, the case gathering dust.

Finally, one day I was staring at the thing and thought, *Fuck it*. I'm going to go out and get a record and see if the thing actually still works. I can't say what inspired the change in me…nostalgia, maybe. Or maybe it was fate. Because that was the day I walked into K-Records and into Otto's life.

I lift the case, gingerly put the album on, and set the needle down. It spins a second before it catches and starts to play.

"Holy *shit*," Otto says. "Is this…*the album?*"

"You bet your ass."

"Oh my god. This is perfect. This night is. Fucking. Perfect."

I put my hands on my hips, feeling pleased with myself. "Surprise."

He's grinning ear to ear. "Come here."

I come closer, and I yelp when he sweeps me off my feet, scooping me into his lap. "You're a saint," he tells me. "Do you know that?"

"Does that mean I have to save your soul?"

"Too late for that," Diego says.

Otto grabs a throw pillow and tosses it at him. It only sends Milo running.

"Hey!" Diego says. "Watch the cat!"

Otto takes the back of my head in his hand—such strong hands—and I melt into his grip. "Thank you," he says sincerely.

He pulls me into a kiss. His lips are soft. Reverent.

Until he bites my bottom lip. I chuckle.

The tea kettle hisses.

"Do you want me to get that?" Diego offers.

"No, I've got it." I put my hand on Otto's chest and push off from his body. He grunts. "Be good," I tell him and muss his hair on my way to the kitchen.

I fix Otto's tea just the way he likes it—black tea and a splash of milk. Diego and Otto chat as I grab some lemon juice from the fridge.

"Diego, want a poor man's hot toddy?"

"Oh. Hell yeah."

I shove aside the clutter on the coffee table and set the three mugs down. I'm not nearly organized enough for a wine rack, but I do have an assortment of bottles shoved underneath the coffee table. I pick up the Bulleit whiskey, pop it open, and tip it to Diego's mug. "Say when."

He watches it carefully, then says, "When."

Another thing I like about Diego—he's a solid guy. He can *drink* and barely feel it. It makes me less self-conscious around Otto, who doesn't drink because of his condition, even though he's said countless times that he doesn't mind if I partake.

I take a sip. It warms me down my throat and into my chest. And *this* feels good. Like taking-off-your-bra-at-the-end-of-the-day good. I'm still high from the thrill of the concert, my ears blown, my pussy wrecked, my blood on fire. I need to come down with the easy music on the record, a toasty drink, and good company.

I lean into my spot beside Diego. My leg brushes against his as I get comfortable, but he doesn't pull back. "Let's play a game."

Diego perks up. "What kind of game?"

"Never Have I Ever?"

"Remind me the rules?" Diego says.

"You say *Never Have I Ever*, and then you give an action. If you've done the thing, you have to drink."

"I'll start," Otto interjects. "Never Have I Ever orgasmed in a crowded room."

"Too soon," I say and take a sip.

Diego chuckles.

When I see that Otto hasn't touched his tea, I chastise, "Otto. Drink."

He knits his eyebrows at me. "I haven't."

I raise my eyebrows. "*The Carousel Bar?*"

"Oh." He grins sheepishly. "Right."

He takes a sip.

I switch it up. Maybe it's the booze, or the music, or just the vibes of the night, but I feel like being bold. So I say, "Never Have I Ever met my soul mate."

I drink. I stare fixedly at Otto.

He *does not drink*.

My mouth twists in a frown.

Otto lifts his hand. "I have an addendum."

"It better be a damn good one, because I'm two seconds away from kicking you out of this apartment."

"Okay, I don't *believe* in soul mates. So how can I find something I don't believe? That's like asking me if I've ever met Santa."

"Why don't you believe in soul mates?" Diego asks conversationally. Diego—bless him—is far more patient than I am.

"The idea that there's one person for everyone?" Otto shakes his head. "No. It's depressing. What if you never meet your soul mate? What if they live all the way across the world? Worse, what if they die? Then what? Then you're screwed?"

"Then you fall in love again," I counter. "But you only get one soul mate."

The corner of Otto's mouth pinches at that. "I think people are varying shades of compatibility."

I roll my eyes. Hard. "Do you hear that, Diego? Romance isn't dead. Otto and I are a *shade of compatibility*."

Diego gives Otto a look. "Dude."

"Now," Otto says—and I can tell he's getting worked up, because he leans in closer and starts gesturing with his hands, "if you'd said *Never Had I Ever found the person I want to spend the rest of my life with*, then yes, I'd have had to drink."

I narrow my eyes at him. It's a start, but it's still not *exactly* what I want to hear.

Still. I can't punish him for being honest. That's what attracted me to him in the first place, isn't it? "Thin ice," I tell him.

Diego takes a swallow from his mug and defuses the situation with "Okay. My turn." He clears his throat. "Never Have I Ever had sex."

I blink at him. If his goal was to distract me from doghousing Otto—well. It worked. Because that throws me. "What? You're a virgin?"

He nods. The mug looks small as he cradles it in both large hands. "Yep."

He's a little awkward but not embarrassed. Just stating a fact.

"For religious reasons?" I pry. "Or…?"

"No, nothing like that." He glances down, pets his thumb over the curved handle of the mug. "I'm open to it. It just… hasn't felt right. Not yet, anyway."

"Okay," Otto says. "Never Have I Ever—"

I hold up a *wait* finger. But my eyes don't leave Diego's. *We're not finished here.*

"Have you ever kissed someone?" I ask him.

Again, he shakes his head. "No."

I set my mug down on the table. "Do you want to?"

My question hangs in the air between us. Diego looks at me, surprised. I can see his brain working over the question. I can see the moment he thinks *yes*, when his eyes dip down to my mouth. When his tongue accidentally betrays him and licks his lips.

And then I see the moment where he thinks *no*. When he remembers where he is, when his eyes panic and dart to Otto. He runs his hand over his thigh and clears his throat.

"I. Uh."

Angel boy is stuck in limbo. So I make the choice for both of us.

I don't know *why* I do it. Maybe I'm punishing Otto for

his *soul mate* comment. Maybe I'm oversexed and worked up from getting teased with my toy all day. Maybe, some nights, I've thought about Diego's rough hands and thick body on top of mine. Maybe this is just a long time coming, something Otto and I have communicated about in our own way, through side-glances and dangerous smiles.

Or maybe Diego is so sweet, such a good guy, and I want to know what an angel's first kiss tastes like.

I take his face, pull him closer, and catch his mouth with my own.

He freezes at first. But he doesn't pull away.

He leans in. His lips are soft, full, and warm. He's not gentle the way I thought he would be. His want is heavy, and he pushes his mouth against mine. It's clumsy and hungry, and I moan into it. He's as delicious as the whiskey, a heat that pours from my lips down the center of my body.

He breaks apart, dipping his chin down. He takes a breath.

"Do you want me to stop?" I ask.

He turns to Otto, those big eyes questioning. "Is this okay?"

Now, I turn to Otto, too. He's staring at us. I know that look in his eyes. It's a dark, piercing look. The look he gives right before he rips my panties off and pounds me hard enough to make me scream.

A little angry.

A little possessive.

A *lot* aroused.

"If it's okay with her, it's okay with me." Otto runs his hand up his thigh. I can see the thickness of him. The shadowed outline of his stiffening cock in those tight pants.

The primal way he's watching us…I feel yearning pull through me like a thread plucked from my heart and down through my cunt, where it gets tight and taut.

I want more of it.

I take Diego's mug from his hands and set it down on the table. No accidents. Not yet, anyway. I straddle Diego, and he lets me, resting his hands on my thighs.

"Do you want to kiss me again?" I ask him. I feel my hair tumble down my back, tickling my shoulders.

"Uh-huh," Diego says. Then his eyes meet mine. He swallows, and I see his Adam's apple bob as he remembers his words. "Yes," he says, clearly this time. Firm. "I do."

I tilt my head and brush my lips against his. This time, his grip squeezes my thighs. I invite him inside, and he takes it, pushing his tongue in my mouth. Hungry, sloppy explorations that feel simultaneously so innocent and so filthy.

"Slower," I whisper against his mouth. "Like this."

I open his mouth with mine, but I don't enter right away. I nibble his bottom lip. Brush my mouth featherlight on his. Then, slowly, I caress his hot tongue with my own.

My palm rests on his chest for balance. His heart is beating so fast against my hand.

Is there a wicked part of me that gets off on corrupting this sweet boy?

Yeah. Maybe.

I flick the tip of my tongue against his, and he shivers. The reaction makes me smile.

Then he does something unexpected.

He cups the back of my head in his hand and roughly plunges his tongue in my mouth. It's a move that takes the breath out of my lungs.

Maybe I was wrong. Maybe this sweet boy is going to corrupt *me* before the night is over.

When we finally break apart, we're both panting. My lips are swollen and wet with him.

My eyes flicker to Otto. I'm not going to lie—I nearly forgot he was there. He's so still, so calm, and there's something infuriating about how collected he is.

I want him to get up, grab me by the hair, and tell me to

stop playing games. I want him to push me to the floor and claim me.

Instead, he waits. And watches. Not a lion, but a panther. Observing.

"You want to touch her, don't you?" Otto asks. His voice is a dark, smoky murmur.

"Uh…" Poor Diego. Always hunting for permission.

"Go ahead. Put your hand in her panties."

His brown eyes meet mine, hunting for consent. I give him a small nod. "It's okay…"

I lift my hips slightly, digging my knees into the couch, and unbutton my jeans, pulling down the zipper.

He wets his lips, then slips his hand in my pants. Over the panties, first, he cups my sex. I gasp; my toy made a mess of me, and the fabric is completely soaked. Diego swallows, and I love seeing the way my arousal turns him on. He watches my face, though, as he pushes my panties to the side and his fingers fumble over my slick pussy.

"Fuck…" Diego moans, and the swear sounds are reverent on his lips. He touches me, exploring, running his fingers over my slit. He traces my hole and moves upward, finding that bundle of nerves. I jerk, because I'm so, so sensitive from my orgasms at the club, and his touch is rough.

"Gently, please," I beg. He lightens his touch and slowly brushes against my clit. Then back down, teasing my entrance.

Otto's eyes are alight. "She's a good little slut, isn't she?"

Diego enters me then, twisting his finger inside of me. I whimper. And that sound—finally—breaks Otto's composure. His lips part just slightly, and I see him intake a quick breath.

And then it's like a switch flips. He can't sit still anymore. He gets to his feet and steps behind me. His hand encircles my throat, and he pulls upward so my head is pressed back against his stomach and I'm looking up at him.

"God, you two are so sweet," Otto says. His thumb pets underneath my chin, and the way he's looking at me makes me want to purr.

He tilts down and sucks my bottom lip, pulling it between his teeth.

"So fucking sweet," he sighs.

Then he plants his hand on the back of the couch, tilts down, and closes his mouth over Diego's.

I freeze for a second. Otto is a *do first, ask for permission later* kind of guy. Which, most of the time, is hot, but I've adopted Diego now—Diego is mine, and I'm not going to let him push Diego into places he's not ready to go.

But Diego doesn't look uncomfortable. The opposite. He clutches Otto's shirt, pulling him in closer, and moans heatedly into the other man's mouth.

When they break apart, Diego has big, soft puppy eyes.

"Is this…?" Diego clears his throat. "Um…"

"If you ask if this is okay one more time, I'm going to slap you," Otto says. "I want to fuck the both of you so bad, I'm going to lose my mind."

And sometimes, Otto just *says the thing* that's on everyone's mind, and I'm so grateful for his unpolished honesty in that moment.

Otto's hand travels roughly, thoughtlessly, down my body. He cups my tit, squeezes, and palms my belly. Meanwhile, his mouth leaves angry kisses down Diego's neck, and I feel Diego's hips give a small, involuntary jerk upward.

"Let's get you out of these," Otto murmurs and moves both hands to yank at my pants.

I shift to stand on the floor so I don't have to do gymnastics to get out of my clothes. Otto helps me out of my pants and my panties and, once I'm bare, gives my ass a stinging slap. It wakes me up, and I squeak.

"Tell him what you want," Otto demands.

I crawl back into Diego's lap, and he turns his hungry

gaze to me. I'm the object of both men's affections tonight… and it's erotic as hell.

I cup his face in my hands, and I tell him, "I want you inside of me."

Diego nods. "I want it, too."

I feel Otto's strong, hard body against my back. He wraps an arm around me, getting between us, and palms Diego's erection briefly through his pants before unzipping them.

"He's big, sunshine," Otto murmurs in my ear, his breath hot. "He's going to split you in half."

I shiver, already throbbing at the thought, fear and excitement tingling through me.

It's Otto who helps pull Diego's cock free from his pants, who gives his friend a couple of generous warm-up strokes.

Diego gasps. "Do you have…um…"

His eyes are wide. He glances at me, then Otto, then back at me. I see him struggling with the question, but he doesn't seem to know how to get it out.

Otto seems to read his friend's mind.

"Would you feel better with a condom?" Otto asks.

"Yeah." Diego blushes. "Sorry if that's…unsexy…"

"Hey." I take Diego's jaw in my hand. "Never apologize for asking for what you want." I grin. "Besides. Call me a freak—"

"You're a freak," Otto breathes against the back of my neck.

"—but my favorite part of Christmas was always *wrapping* my gifts."

Relief passes over his face, and his bones relax. Otto kisses the side of my neck and then pulls back.

"Stay here," Otto says. He walks away, and he's gone for only a couple of seconds. When he comes back, he has a condom in hand. He's got the packet pinched between his fingers, and he holds it out to me. "Want to do the honors?"

"Yes, please."

I'll be honest—Otto and I haven't used condoms in months, so I'm not even sure where he found that one. I wear an IUD, and we both got tested when we started dating, with the contingency that we'd get tested again if anyone *else* came into our mix.

And it's been lovely. And fun. But there is something wonderfully erotic about putting a condom on a guy. I take it out of the wrapper, position it over the tip of him, and slowly roll it on.

As I fix it over Diego, I feel Otto move behind me. He unzips his pants and then rubs his cock between my legs. I moan as his hard organ rubs against my slit, the friction sending bolts of pleasure through me. My hand gets distracted, and I stroke Diego, badly wanting someone inside of me. It takes a moment before I realize Otto is lubricating himself with my arousal, and the thought makes my throat dry.

"Otto," I whine.

"Take him," Otto demands. "Then take me."

I get close to Diego and feel the head of him press against me. I shudder because Otto wasn't wrong—he's thick. I'm dripping wet, my lust reignited with Diego's sweet kisses and Otto's rough touches, and there's a push and then I lower all the way down, taking him fully inside of me.

"Oh my god," Diego moans. The sound is so sweet coming from his lips. His eyebrows furrow, eyes squeezed shut for a moment to take in the sensation.

I need a second, too. It's overwhelming. I've been tormented with pleasure all day from the vibrator, but *this* is different. Diego is blood-hot and steel-hard, and he fills me so sweetly.

Then Otto nestles in behind me. His fingers press inside me first, and then he nudges his cock against my asshole. We've done this before, but I still have to brace myself when he pushes it inside of me.

I whine and clutch Diego's shoulders. "Oh god…"

They're *both* inside of me now. I'm so full…and it feels so perfect.

Otto's hand grips my thick hair tightly. It pulls against my scalp and makes me gasp. "No one told you to stop," Otto says. "Ride him."

I whimper and obey. I'm a bad bitch in the streets—but for Otto?

I'll be his submissive slave in the sheets.

I rock back and forth, undulating over Diego. I let him slip out, just a little, and then rock back, taking him deeper inside of me. The feeling of his thickness and Otto's rubbing my inner walls is exquisite, and I can't get enough of it.

I drop my head forward, and my forehead touches Diego's. We pant together, and his breath is warm on my lips. I feel so connected to him, and to Otto, and my head spins with it.

"God, you two are beautiful," Otto says, his voice thick with want. "So fucking hot. Tell him you love his cock."

"I love your cock!"

"Tell him you love the way it feels."

"I love the way…*oh god*. It's so good…"

I'm losing control, and so is Diego. He's gone quiet, twitching, his grip at my hips relaxing, then tightening, then relaxing again. He's struggling to keep himself together, and there's honestly something so hot about watching him fighting his body's impulses underneath me.

Otto notices, too. With the hand that's not gripping my hair, he reaches forward and slips his fingers gently through Diego's tight, dark curls.

Rough with me. Gentle with Diego.

"Hey," Otto says, a breathy murmur, "don't kill yourself. You're trapped with us now, which means you're going to cum, like, a million times tonight. Don't sweat it if you can't hold back."

And, honestly, it warms me to see the way Otto is with Diego.

He's filthy with me. Rough and cruel. Because he *knows* that's what I like—and I know anything said in the bedroom is just play; it's not real.

But he's different with Diego. Sweet. Patient. Because that's what Diego needs.

If Otto is good at anything, he's good at reading people and giving them *exactly* what they need. Dangerously good. He actually cares about people. Wants them to be happy. If he ever decided to go into politics, he could probably rule the world.

Diego and I are just lucky to exist in his orbit.

"Oh, fuck," Diego whimpers. Then his hands cover his eyes, and his cheeks flush. It's his first time cumming in front of people—*two people*—and I don't blame him for needing to hide, that lick of shame that comes from too much pleasure. "Fuck," he repeats, "fuck, fuck, *fuck*."

I kiss the back of his hand, right on the club stamp, and I murmur, "Please, Diego. Give it to me."

The permission unravels him. He swells and twitches inside of me, spilling, filling the condom. His moan is deep and long, and the sound sends me spinning.

I curl up against him and whine. My angry, abused cunt gives hard, intense pulses, and I moan and squirm in Diego's lap, against Otto's hips, rutting my way through my painfully good orgasm.

It's blinding. Like white snow in the morning. I catch my breath, my mind hazy, like I've just stepped into a dream.

Otto presses a kiss to the side of my throat. He pulls his cock, still unspent, out of me, and I whimper, feeling emptier with him.

"You two are perfect together," Otto says. "Do you know that?"

"The three of us, you mean," Diego says, and I have to agree.

Otto pulls his pants up his hips, zipper still hanging open.

"I'm gonna wash up," Otto says. "You two get in bed."

I watch as he hops past the coffee table. He stops, however, to pick up his mug of tea and drains it.

I crinkle my nose. "Tea? At a time like this?"

"It's almost cold," he complains, as though that's a crime.

I chuckle, and he exits, heading to the bathroom.

Now it's just the two of us, and we catch our breath. I slip my hand over Diego's hair and pet the small, spiky hairs at the back of his neck as he softens inside of me.

"Is it really okay if I stay?" he asks.

"I hate to break it to you, but you missed the train a looooong time ago."

He laughs lightly. "Yeah. I guess." Then his eyes move behind me. "I think we traumatized your cat."

I glance over my shoulder and see Milo tucked behind my potted snake plant.

"Milo!" I tell him. "It's okay! It was all consensual, I promise!"

Milo reaches up a paw and bats the plant.

Diego is grinning now. It's really nice to see from the man who is normally so stoic and serious.

He shifts out of me, and I groan. I'm far too empty now. My cunt is sore, but I'm giddy, savoring that afterglow.

I reach between us and slip the condom off Diego's softening organ. It's heavy with him, and I pinch it between my fingers. It's a strange pride, knowing he came this hard *for me*.

Almost seems a shame to drop it in the waste bin, but I do. Then I tiptoe my fingers across his chest. "Do you wanna see my bedroom?"

"Yeah," he says. "Lead the way."

Then he surprises me and lifts me up, carrying me in his

arms. I yelp, then laugh, hooking my legs around his waist. I point down the hall. "That way."

Diego carries me through my small apartment, around the corner, and into my bedroom. I wish I'd thought ahead, but honestly, it'd probably take a week to clean my bedroom. There are clothes, shopping bags, hangers, and cat toys scattered on every inch of the place. Diego politely steps into the few bare spaces of floor before setting me down on my bed.

I take off my shirt and bra and add them to the pile on the floor. Fully naked now, I sit up in bed and open my arms.

"Come," I say. "I need skin."

"Spoken like a serial killer," Diego says. But he takes off his clothes, until he's standing completely naked in front of me.

I let my eyes roam over him. He has a gorgeous body. Brown skin, strong arms, soft stomach.

He does the same, pouring over me with his eyes. "You're a vision," he tells me.

I can't help but smile. "Kiss me."

Diego climbs into bed. He pulls me against him, cradling me, and catches my lips in his own. My apartment is cold—fucking New York City winters are relentless, and my heater is trash. I've got goose bumps, my dark nipples hard on his chest, but his body is furnace-hot, and I can't get enough of it.

His kisses are unpracticed but not exactly innocent—curious, exploring. We savor each other now, sweetly tasting one another.

I soak in his gentleness like a vampire.

Then I hear Otto's voice. "This," he says, "is exactly what I was hoping to walk in on."

8

DIEGO

Otto emerges from the adjoining bathroom. The backlight haloes him.

He's wearing his jeans but nothing else. He has the muscles of a man whose body betrayed him when he was younger and, now, he's worked twice as hard to beat it into submission. He's ripped, a level of self-control I couldn't possibly pull off, with strong biceps and a tight stomach.

Then there's that pink, crescent-shaped scar that swoops across his hip and vanishes under his jeans. He strips so he's completely naked, too, and now I can see the full new moon scar.

It's his warrior scar. Or, as Otto likes to joke, "I survived a kidney transplant, and all I got was this dumb scar."

He's carrying a bottle of clear liquid, and he sets it on the bedside table.

Then he takes Naomi by the hips, yanks her closer, and climbs into bed on top of her. Her legs wrap around him and they tangle up together.

"Did Diego fuck you good, baby girl?" Otto asks her.

"Yeah..." Her eyes are half-lidded. She reaches between them and takes him in her hand. He hardens to her touch.

I like watching them together. The way they are in the bedroom just feels like an extension of who they are in public—playful, sensual, and wildly obsessed with each other. They touch each other easily, as though they've memorized every inch of the other's body.

Otto moves his hand between her legs and pinches the delicate, dark skin of her labia between his thumb and forefinger. "Your poor cunt," he taunts. "She's taken quite the beating today, hasn't she? Must be worn raw."

Naomi mewls and squirms, and as I watch the two of them play, my heartbeat picks up, a thudding in my chest and in my cock.

"Please—*fuck*—it's so sensitive."

"Kiss first."

She kisses Otto hard, desperate, and his tongue mixes with hers. Then he releases his grip on her swollen sex, and she sighs.

Otto's eyes meet mine. It's like being pierced through with an arrow, the way his blue eyes catch. "Good girl," he says to Naomi. "Now stay."

Then he shifts a whole couple inches over in the small bed and climbs over me, straddling my thighs and pinning me down.

"You have fun?" he asks.

"Yeah…"

"Yeah?" He says it like a challenge.

My throat closes. I can only confirm with "Uh-huh."

He chuckles low in his throat, the way a jungle cat might purr. Appropriate, because I feel like a mouse caught in his claws.

Naomi is perfect. Naomi is beautiful and bold. Badass and adorable. A goddess.

My mom would've loved her. Call it heteronormative trauma, but that's a thought I can't get out of my head, even now. It's not a bad thought, either. It's a warm thought. The duet of women's laughter. Mom stuffing Naomi's pockets with recipe clippings. That spark in mom's eyes, words unsaid: *I knew you'd pick a good one.*

But Otto's eyes meet mine, and it's like a violin string has been plucked deep inside of me. It hums and quivers. I've wanted him since before I had words to articulate what that *want* meant.

The *want* isn't sexual, exactly (though it's not, *not* sexual, either). It's more than that.

I crave him the way a sailboat craves wide-open sea.

I crave him the way a moonflower craves unbroken night.

This desire is natural, inevitable, fated.

We had to end up here. It had to circle back to Otto

His mouth connects with mine—*almost*—lips grazing my skin. A whisper of a kiss.

"I like kissing you," he says.

"Yeah," I murmur. "Me too."

His mouth quirks in a grin. "Wicked." He takes my consent and finally seals me into his kiss. I push back, wanting too much—I can feel myself pressing too hard, too desperate, but I can't seem to stop myself.

Otto chuckles. It's a puff of hot air against my mouth.

"Relax," he says. "You think you can do that for me? Relax?"

"I can try."

"I would. I want to be inside of you…and it's going to hurt if you aren't relaxed."

My face stings, like the smart of a winter's chill, except everything in me is hot.

Those blue eyes hunt mine. Searching. "Is that what you want?"

He doesn't take me with the same reckless boldness he uses with Naomi.

But they've been doing this for a long time. Otto and me…we're just learning each other.

The fact that he takes the time to make sure we're both on the same page means more than he knows.

I nod and shift on my back, adjusting up on my elbows.

"Yeah," I confirm, "I want it. Just tell me what to do."

I'm trying to sound casual. Trying to sound like I know what I'm doing. Trying to sound like I'm not completely lost at sea.

"Can you pass me the lube, beautiful? And a condom."

Naomi, who has been curled on her side like a content cat, watching us, unfurls now. She takes the bottle off the bedside table and rummages around a small drawer until she finds what she's looking for. She hands both the wrapper and bottle over to Otto.

"Good girl," Otto says, and I can tell that phrase melts her. He cups the back of her head and pulls her into a loving, lingering kiss.

Watching them together…it's a beautiful thing. Anyone can see how much she trusts him. How much he loves her.

He takes the items from her. Otto tosses the condom, and it lands softly on my stomach.

"Hold on to that, baby," he tells me. "I'll let you know when I need it."

Baby. That's a new one.

Not at all a word anyone has used for a big, grown-ass man like me.

I snort on a laugh. "Did you just call a grown man *baby*?"

Otto retorts, "Did you like it?"

"…Yeah, kinda."

I take the wrapped condom and hold it in my hand. It feels good to have a job. It feels good to do *something* with my hands.

Otto grins.

"You're doing great, baby."

Otto squeezes out some lube onto his fingertips. He rubs his hands together, pops the bottle shut, and sets it aside. I watch his hand dip between my legs and then I feel it. It's cold at first and my breath catches even though I should be prepared—I'm a doctor; I literally use the stuff *all the time*. It is strangely clinical at first, the way Otto pushes the lube around my hole before finally plunging his finger in.

I bite the inside of my lip. I screw my eyes shut. He moves a finger around, testing me, and then presses a second finger inside.

"*Oh*," I say. My voice shudders.

He doesn't say *are you okay?* Or *do you need me to stop?*

He knows I'll tell him if I need to.

He just says, "I know."

And he *does*. He does know. He knows everything I need and everything I want.

Even before I know I want it.

He proves it with his fingers, turning them and stroking someplace deep inside of me. It feels strange at first and then warm, and then the warmth blossoms into *really fucking good*. I gasp. The condom wrapper crinkles when my hand fists around it, and I feel my cock surge in my lap.

"That's the spot," Otto says, his voice velvet and deep, "isn't it?"

I don't *know* what he means, exactly. But I feel it. As though all of my focus on concentration is zeroed in the smallest little strokes of his fingers.

"Uh-huh…" My own voice is barely a grunt.

My heels dig into the mattress. It takes everything within me to keep myself together.

But Otto doesn't let me settle into my pleasure. He ramps it up. One hand massages inside of me while he wraps his other hand around my cock. His palm is slick with the lube, and I slide through his fingers easily as he pumps me.

"Jesus," I say. "*Fuck*."

I've lost control of my tongue. Among other things. I'm moaning now, lifting my hips to meet his touch. He strokes me boldly, exploring the ridges of me, the tip, and back down, squeezing the base. It's not long before I'm shuddering, jerking into his ministrations.

"You're ready for me, aren't you?" Otto asks.

I *completely* forgot I was holding on to the condom. I remember it now and open up my palm. I hold it up in offering.

"Please," I say.

I'm surprised by the word. I'm surprised by the heat in my voice.

I'm surprised by the way Otto's eyes briefly widen and then go *fucking feral*.

He takes the offering from my palm, rips it between his fingers and his teeth, and quickly slides it over his length. Then he positions himself between my legs, locks his eyes with mine, and…

I feel him. The meaty head of him. Seeking. I tense up, bracing, and knot my fingers in the sheets below me.

"Relax," Otto tells me. "Breathe. You could take my fingers, you can take my prick."

It's the reminder I need. I swallow. I try to breathe.

But when he pushes inside, it still hurts.

I grit my teeth. Immediately, Naomi is beside me. Her nails trace through my hair. Gently, she kisses my shoulder. "Are you okay?" she asks.

"Uh-huh." Tight, shallow breaths.

Otto pauses. "You want me to stop?"

I shake my head. My neck is hot. My cheeks and ears are burning.

"Just do it," I tell him firmly. "All the way."

The only thing worse than this pain is the slow build of anticipation. I'm pragmatic. I need to know what I'm dealing with.

I feel Otto's hand at my hip, and at my request, he slams his hips forward.

That takes the breath out of me.

He's inside me now. *Deep*. It feels like he's rearranging my insides.

I bite my hand and growl into it. I can't help it. It keeps me from screaming out, anyway.

"Okay," I say when I finally have enough air in my lungs to breathe. "Just…hold that. Just a second. I just need a second."

"Take all the time you need, baby," Otto encourages. "We've got all night."

I try to relax, but it's hard when all I can feel is the throbbingly tight stretch around Otto. I try to focus on Naomi's gentle kisses. The featherlight touches of Otto's fingertips as they trace down my abdomen. He pets the hair at my happy trail.

"You're such a beast," he tells me, out of the blue.

I can't help but snort at that. "A *beast*? That's kinda racist, man."

"I mean…you're powerful." He thinks about his words. "You're a king."

I bite back a smile. Because *king* does sound nice on his lips.

Then his fingertips find my cock, and I gasp. It's just a light touch, grazing from base to tip. I've softened slightly in my struggle to relax, but he barely touches me and suddenly I'm painfully rigid again.

Otto takes the lead again. He wraps me in his hand and strokes me, slowly.

Now I can't help the moan that leaves me. I find myself rocking into his touch and, subsequently, moving him inside of me.

Things that felt bad now start to feel good.

Really good.

Otto picks up on it immediately. "Feels good, doesn't it?"

"Yeah…"

"I'm going to fuck you now. Tell me if it's too much."

With that, Otto adjusts his body so he's hovering over me, a hand planted by my head. He moves his hips now, thrusting them, while he keeps touching me, stroking me, coaxing me further and further away from sanity.

My arms unlock from my sides, and I grab him. I grip his shoulders. Dig my fingers into the skin on his back.

Two seconds ago, my body was fighting him. Now, I can't get enough. I want him deeper. Closer. *More*.

Naomi nibbles my ear. "Good boy," she whispers, and I shudder.

It's overwhelming. All of this pleasure. All of this affection.

It starts to build in me again. Swelling. Tightening. Until I feel like my body is taut and humming with ecstasy. Teetering on that sweet, terrifying precipice.

Things like tears and pain have always been a private thing for me. A rule in our house was *don't ever let them see you hurt.* So it stands to reason that when I'm drowning in pleasure, I resort to my old coping mechanisms—run and hide.

I cover my face. I put my arms over my eyes. I bite my lip to swallow back a moan.

But he finds me. I hide. He seeks.

"Nope," Otto says. "None of that."

He takes my arm and pins it over my head. I'm stronger than Otto. I can push back if I want. But I don't want to. I want to be vulnerable. I want to break.

I gasp and choke on my pleasure. My face feels hot, and I'm sure it's not pretty. I'm sure I look like a mess. I screw my eyes shut and—

"No again," Otto says. "Look at me."

I force my eyes open. Those sparkling blues look down at me.

"Oh god," I whisper.

"I know."

"Oh...*god*...!"

"*I know*. Cum for me, king."

I explode. It pulls an inhumane noise from me—some deep sound that has been tucked away at the bottom of my lungs and only now has the strength to come out. I grip the mattress, twist. I shiver, writhe, and I grab the back of his neck and anchor myself to him.

I throb, and Otto strokes me through it, wringing every drop of my orgasm from me. My eyes don't leave his—not once. I watch as his jaw tenses, his breath catches, and he gives a low, relieved sigh. His hips buck once, and he empties inside of me.

"*Fuck*," he swears, so quietly under his breath, and that small word tingles through my entire body.

He folds over me, and his lips brush mine. I lean in to kiss him back like a man starving, but—

He pulls away. A whimper leaves my lips before I can stop it.

"C'mere, baby," Otto says and closes his hand over the back of Naomi's head. He pushes her down and says, "Kiss Diego."

Naomi curls up beside me. Her warmth feels so nice. Her lips are so soft. She strokes her fingers through my hair, and her nails scrape across my scalp. It sends a shiver through me, and I hear myself choke out a noise—a half sob. Of relief or pain, I'm not sure.

"It's okay," she murmurs gently to me as she covers my face in kisses. "You did so good, baby. So good."

Her fingertips trail down my neck, my chest. She's so soft, and it makes me soft in turn.

I'm coming off my high. I'm sweaty and kiss-drunk and so, so spent.

"I'm going to pull out of you," Otto says. "Is that okay?"

"Yeah," I grunt. The fullness of him is starting to get uncomfortable again.

He eases out of me, and I exhale slowly as he does. It's the strangest sensation, and I feel so goddamn empty afterward.

Empty and sticky. I can try to hide behind my hands, but I've covered my belly with evidence of just how much I *enjoyed* all of that.

I feel drunk on both of them. But I need to reorient myself.

"I need to clean up," I say.

Naomi points to the bathroom door left ajar. I untangle myself from the two of them, and they fall back together like liquid, filling in the spaces I left empty.

I have to nudge a pink sweater on the floor out of the way with my toes in order to close the door behind me.

It's quiet in here. The bathroom floor is tiled and cold under my bare feet.

I've always been a solitary guy. I've only ever needed two or three close friends. I do better one-on-one with people than in a crowd. I don't mind being alone.

So even though the sex was powerful and intimate, it was also overwhelming, and I need a minute with myself to wrap my brain around what just happened.

Naomi has a lot of beauty products partially spilled across her tiny bathroom sink. The counter is half glitter. I take the washcloth that looks the most worn down, wet it, and start cleaning myself up. My belly is striped with my own cum, my cock slick with lube and Naomi, and I sponge-bath myself clean.

Slowly, the orgasmic haze starts to clear. Now that I'm alone with my thoughts, I can feel the unease, like a rock sitting on my chest.

Something's nagging at me. Something's not right.

It's the way Otto pulled away. When I needed him most—

when I'd come apart underneath him, sticky and covered in both of us—he pulled away.

He gave me to Naomi instead.

It shouldn't bother me. I tell myself I'm thinking too hard about it. I need to stop plucking at the stray thread, or I'll unravel the entire, beautiful night.

I come up with excuses for him. Maybe it was innocent. Maybe he was trying to connect us. Bring the three of us together.

But something about it still feels off. I can't put my finger on it.

9

OTTO

I shift onto my back and half sit up against the wall behind Naomi's bed.

She curls up against me like a kitten.

Her head rests on my shoulder, her hand on my stomach, and—

I wince.

I'm satisfied. Elated. I fucked hard. I came hard. I loved every second of it.

But I'm also in pain. A stabbing pain low in my belly that picks away at my comfort.

I can't tell Diego. He'd panic. I can't tell Naomi. She wouldn't get it. Hell, I can't even admit it to *myself*—because we still have fifteen minutes until midnight, and I just need to make it that long.

I need my perfect, unspoiled night.

"I love you," Naomi says suddenly. And it throws me. Because we haven't shared those words—not ever—and for her to say them now when I'm grinding against my molars…

It throws me through a loop.

"What?"

I know that's not what someone wants to hear when they

first confess their love. But I need a minute to reorient myself.

Naomi moves her hand off my stomach and settles it on my chest. The pain is less there, and when she looks into my eyes, the throbbing ache is almost completely gone.

I could lose myself in those soft, brown eyes.

"I love you, Otto Stratton," she says with as much conviction as she can.

And my heart breaks for it.

I need to tell her: *I'm not the guy you make lifetime commitments with.*

I need to tell her: *I just don't think I'm going to be around that long.*

I need to tell her: *My kidney's failing. My body is failing. I'm failing.*

I need to tell her: *Run*.

But Naomi is looking at me. Those beautiful eyes. Those *brave* eyes. She's the bravest woman I know. Her body fits perfectly against mine, her breasts against my arm, her pelvis on my hip, my leg wedged between hers. The room smells like sex, heavy and musky, with a hint of the incense she burns. Outside her window, draped with heavy purple curtains on either side, a fresh dusting of snow falls.

In this moment, I'm weak.

"I love you, too," I tell her.

She smiles. It's a smile that warms me from the inside out.

She draws herself up just enough to press her lips to mine. When we kiss, it's slow and gentle, and I feel like I can taste her heart spilling out onto my tongue.

And it might be the most selfish thing I've ever said. But right here, right now, it feels right.

PART II

CHRISTMAS EVE. DECEMBER 24TH

10

DIEGO

I don't manage to get out the-thing-I-want-to-say last night.

By the time I came back from the bathroom, Otto and Naomi were curled up in an affectionate pile. I couldn't bring myself to ruin the moment.

I curled up with them. The room was cold, but their body heat was so warm, and I slept better than I've slept in a very, very long time.

I wake up to Milo hacking.

The cat is sitting at the foot of the bed. When I open my eyes, he stares directly at me, hunches, and makes a terrible glugging sound.

I get it. I don't like people in my space, either.

I quickly untangle from Naomi, who has snuggled up between Otto and me. Neither she nor Otto wakes as I scoop up the cat. He dangles from my hand as I carry him outside the room, where he can't make a mess in the bed, and set him down on the hardwood floor.

He glugs a couple more times, hacks, and then spits out a hairball.

Then he looks at me. Blinks.

"You're okay," I tell him and scratch him between the ears. "Happens to all of us."

He burps, then mewls.

I clean up the hairball and find a disinfectant under the sink to wipe up the spot. His food is under there, too, so I fill his empty bowl and change out his water.

He watches me dubiously.

"Are we friends now?" I ask him.

He walks over, sniffs the food, and keeps his eyes on me as he takes a small, dainty bite.

I'll take it.

Remnants of last night are still scattered around Naomi's apartment. I find my briefs and pants and put those on. I pile Naomi and Otto's clothes up on the couch. I move our mugs from the table to the sink and rinse them out. Naomi has a coffee machine, so I fill it with water, replace the filter, and get a pot going. Now the room smells less like disgruntled cat and more like morning brew.

I open up Naomi's cabinet and find myself stumped. She and her roommate have a full shelf of mugs. All of them novelty, no two mugs look the same.

This is a problem for me, because I don't know if any of these are sacred and not to be used. I, for one, have a hand-painted mug at home. I made it when I was a kid—with Otto, actually. We spent a summer going to art class together, I think to give our parents a couple of hours of child-free time. I came home with a lopsided ceramic mug with flames painted up and down the sides, like it was a hot rod.

Mom cherished it. It was her favorite mug, so now it's my favorite mug. And I don't let anyone else drink from it; even Otto knows to steer clear. House rule.

I try to find the mug that looks least likely to have some sentimental value. It's a plain mud-brown mug that might've been picked up from an art market. I'm craving the outside, so once I make sure Milo is a safe distance away, I take my mug of coffee and open the window so I can step out to the fire escape, closing the window behind me.

It's bitterly cold here. But less cold, somehow, than Hannsett Island. It's the humidity—everything is so wet on Hannsett. It's that cold that soaks right through you. This is a dry, breath-stealing cold.

I like it, though. It wakes me up. The black metal of the fire escape is coated in snow, and it crunches under my bare feet. The coffee is watery but warms my throat. I lean over the railing, sip my coffee, and let my breath crystalize in front of me as I watch the morning commuters go back and forth on the street below.

I'm not alone for long. The window opens and closes with a hiss. Otto climbs over and stands beside me. He's got a blanket wrapped around his shoulders, burrito-ing. Clutched in his hand, he's got a cup of coffee—a holiday-themed mug with a Santa face on it.

"Good morning," I tell him.

His blanket-puffy shoulder presses against mine. "It's fucking freezing out here."

"That's winter for you."

He shivers dramatically and takes a sip. I try to bite back a smile.

This is easy. Familiar. It feels like we're teenagers again. We've woken up well after noon (after staying up all night watching movies and laughing). Now, we're tired, hair askew, but enjoying that content, zombie-like post-sleepover bliss.

There's nothing better.

"How'd you sleep?" I ask.

"Like the dead." He looks at me, and those eyes look so bright in the morning light. Caribbean blue and serious. "Let's clear the air."

I nod. "Okay."

"Last night," he starts. "Was that okay for you?"

"Yeah. It was."

"Everything you thought your first time would be?"

"Better." I hesitate. I don't want to break up the mood, but I have to say it. "There was…something."

Otto's gaze trains on me. "What kind of something?"

"Not bad, exactly. Just…well." I can't look at him, so I look down at the street. Petals of soft snow fall below. "After I… after *we*. You told me to kiss Naomi."

Otto nods but doesn't interrupt. He just listens, patiently.

"And…while that was nice…I think, in that moment, I needed you."

Otto stares at me. He says nothing, as though he's…thinking.

Why does he feel so far away?

It's killing me. I've never felt this far from him. Not in the nearly twenty years of knowing each other. Last night, we were closer than we've ever been, and now…

Otto catches the back of my head, pulls me in, and his lips meet mine.

Fully. Softly. He doesn't pull away this time. He lingers, and I sigh into his mouth, savoring him.

I was cold. Now, I'm warm again.

"I'm sorry," Otto says. Our lips disconnect, but he's still holding me close. "Better?"

"Yeah," I say. "I think so."

We untangle from each other, but some of the thorns have left my chest.

He's closer, now.

"To clarify, last night was perfect," I reiterate, because I don't want to end this conversation with a bad taste on his tongue. "I'm really glad my first time was with you." A question mark dances over Otto's expression, the morning light touching his long eyelashes. I quickly add, "And Naomi. Both of you."

A small, knowing smile tugs at Otto's lips. He leans

against the fire escape and looks down to the street below thoughtfully.

"You're my bacon, Diego."

He says it so softly, I have to make sure I heard him correctly.

"I'm your...what?"

But then Otto's eyelids drop. He forces them open, but they close again.

He sways lightly on his feet.

The medical professional in me recognizes the signs: blown-out pupils, inability to concentrate, color washed out of the face.

Alarm hits me in waves.

"Hey...are you okay?"

But Otto doesn't answer. He can't.

He loses his grip on his mug. I don't try to save it.

My arms are too busy grabbing him. I catch him just as he collapses, and he sinks into me as he faints, a boneless heap in my arms.

Below us, Santa's face explodes into a million pieces on the sidewalk.

* * *

The blood pressure monitor blinks in a steady line.

Otto is slumped in the hospital bed. We made it to Hannsett Island—but just barely. He could hardly stay conscious on the ferry. I wouldn't have taken him here, except I know...

There are no better doctors.

He's asleep now. He's been pumped with fluids. Stabilized. Naomi sits in the chair next to his bed. She's hasn't left his side.

I watch this all from the window separating us. I'm in the hallway. Beside me, Dr. Donovan paces back and forth.

He's been like this since we got here.

"I don't understand," he says. His voice is curt, tight. "Was he drinking?"

"No," I murmur.

"His potassium and sodium levels shouldn't be this high. His GFR is 10%. This level of degradation doesn't happen overnight."

I wet my lips with my tongue. *The truth will set you free*. "It didn't," I say. "He's been bad. For a long time."

Dr. Donovan stops pacing. His arms fold over his chest, and he stares at me. "Start talking."

I take in a breath. I reach into my pocket and pull out Otto's blood sample results.

11

JASON

*T*hey used to call the operating room an *operating theater*.

I think about that sometimes when I step inside to perform a surgery. It does, in a way, feel like a big performance. Nurses and attendings hovering over the table, nothing but eyes peering out from over their masks. Big, bright lights aimed directly at the main player. Curtains of skin and tissue peel back, and the play begins, organs and bones and blood all serving their part to tell the singular, unique story of one person's life.

I'm the director. The man behind the scenes. God of the operating theater. As the head of surgery, I orchestrate every detail of the surgery, down to the very music we play in the background to keep us alert during five- or six-hour surgeries.

But here, in the filming studio, with bright lights blaring down on me and a thick application of stage makeup, I'm starting to feel like a piece of meat.

There's no audience here—just me, the crew, and a one-eyed camera pointed at me. I speak directly to it, with a smile that's ironed onto my mouth.

"Negativity, like infection, is a toxin," I tell the camera and the millions of unseen people behind it. "It's why we encourage people with terminal illnesses to partake in exercise, yoga, and spiritual healing. Now, do I think positive thinking is a cure for cancer? No. Absolutely not. I'm a doctor, I've been a surgeon for over twenty years, and I want to encourage people to trust their doctors. Get tested as often as you can. With that said—I think science and healing can go hand in hand. We know so much more about that body than we did fifty, twenty, even ten years ago. Yet there's still so much left to discover. I think that positive thinking is more than hooey witchcraft—it's science, it's your brain healing your body.

"Because I'm a doctor, I'm not going to just give you a basic diagnosis and tell you to run with it."

My stage is small—nothing but the lounge chair I'm sitting in and the coffee table next to me. I lift up my book from the table, hard copy, and it's got a picture of me on the front.

"In my book, *Cut Out Negativity*, I go into step-by-step ways to realign your thinking and support healthier attitudes. Buy it for your family, stick it in a stocking—hell, buy it for yourself. Treat yourself. You deserve it."

I wink for the camera. And in that moment, even I think:
I'm a sell-out.

"That's a wrap!" shouts Kerrie. Kerrie is my director of photography and my agent, and with that, the scene cuts. The camera stops rolling, the lights dim, and I can relax my smile.

An assistant comes by to help me unclip the mini microphone from my shirt. Kerrie, all five foot two with bushy brown hair like a cocker spaniel, approaches me. She's got big-eared headphones around her neck, crossed arms, and a pleased smirk.

"Good job, Jason. We'll slap on a couple promotional

graphics and blow the Christmas sales out of the water."

I give her a grin. "Here to please."

The truth is—this isn't where I belong. I experienced a strange bout of "insta-fame" in my thirties. After a TV spot, I suddenly became the face of general surgery. It was a surprise but not a shock—after all, I've practically been bred for this. My family was well-to-do, and if there was anything they imparted on me, it was charisma.

I know how to work an audience. I have my entire life.

Dad, if nothing else, taught me how to own every room I walk into.

You're a King. Act like one.

That was a refrain growing up. I've ditched ninety percent of the toxic shit my father drilled into my head, but that one stuck around.

Kerrie puts her hand on her hip and cocks her head, which I clocked long ago as her *I'm about to ask you to do something* stance. "Hey, what're you doing for Christmas?"

"Ice cream."

"Huh?"

I grin. "It's tradition. Every Christmas, we do a family outing to the ice cream shop."

"All three of you, right? You, Kenzi, and Donovan?"

I press a smile on. "All three of us."

"That's sweet. If the three of you wanted to do a little live Christmas day video…just something quick for the social, nothing huge. I think that'd really go over well."

What she means is: people are obsessed with our family.

I can't blame them. If you'd told the teenager version of myself that I'd have a wife, a husband, and two kids, I'd have probably punched you in the face.

Of course, back then, I was angry, frustrated, didn't know what I wanted, and was confused about the few things I *did* want.

We had a private ceremony off the coast of Hannsett on

our sailboat *Dock Buoy*. And by private, I mean *private*. Besides the three of us, we had our two kids (Otto, fourteen, and Joan, only two), Kenzi's mom and stepdad, our friend Maria, and her son, Diego.

Donovan's parents had passed and, for the sake of my sanity, I'd had to cut my parents clean out of my life. It was one of the hardest things I've ever had to do…and, ultimately, one of the kindest things I've ever done for myself.

We said vows, made promises to each other, and at the end of it, each of us got two rings. Donovan and I have a similar set—elegant stacking bands. Kenzi has two diamond-studded twin bands on her ring finger.

We had cake. We drank wine. And at the end of the night, Maria took the kids for the night, and the small wedding party went back to shore. The three of us spent the rest of the night fucking, eating cake off each other, and jumping in the phosphorescent-glowing water to wash the icing and cum from our bodies.

I remember one particular moment. I was stretched out on the bow of the boat. I was naked and air-drying, and red streaks of dawn stretched out over the sky. Kenzi fell asleep between us, curled up like a cat on Donovan's chest. Donovan was still awake, like me, but we were sharing the silence together. I closed my eyes and listened to the water slosh rhythmically against the side of the boat. The sounds of the anchor chain clicking against the boat. Seagulls in the distance, cawing.

I thought, *Remember this. Remember how happy you are in this moment. When shit gets hard, or people come at you and judge your love, just close your eyes and remember this moment when nothing felt more natural, or true, or real. Remember this, and everything will be okay.*

But I should've known better. As a surgeon, I know the hardest-to-cure ailments are rarely the external forces—a hit-and-run, falling off a roof, that sort of thing. It's the unseen, undiagnosed problems that develop in the shadows for years that really bite you in the ass when they finally come to light.

Donovan and I have always been opposite sides of the same coin. For years, it balanced us. Kept our trio stable. Or at least, I *thought* it did. Until our good friend Maria passed away in March and sent us reeling.

Thanksgiving was the straw that broke the camel's back. Donovan asked for space. We gave it to him. I haven't touched, held, or fucked my husband in nearly a month.

Kenzi and I overcompensate, unable to keep our hands off each other. Our sex is desperate and frenzied. And every now and then, her eyes will wander or my hands will reach for someone who isn't there.

We're emptier without him.

So when Kerrie gives me that wide smile, begging for a happy-holiday Christmas card from my family to the world, I don't know how to tell her that things are complicated right now. That it's going to be hard enough to drag Donovan kicking and screaming for our annual ice cream photo, let alone convince him to pretend everything is fine for the social media audience.

Instead, I just nod and smile. "I'll see what I can do."

The answer seems to satisfy her. "Oh," she adds and reaches into her pocket. She tosses me my phone, and I catch it. "Your phone's been blowing up. You might want to check it. Merry Christmas, Jason."

"Merry Christmas."

I glance down at my phone. Missed calls and texts. All from Donovan.

Thinking of the devil.

When I unlock my screen, however, the messages make my blood turn to ice.

[text: Donovan] Otto is in the hospital
[text: Donovan] Get here when you can

12

OTTO

I'm not supposed to be here.

I open my eyes to off-white walls. The steady beeping of my heart rate monitor. Uncomfortably stiff sheets underneath me and a green hospital robe wrapped around me.

At first I think, *This is a nightmare*.

Most of my nightmares take place in the hospital.

But then I see her. Naomi. She's sitting in the chair beside my bed in sweatpants and a college sweatshirt, her thick dark hair a wild mane around her head. When her eyes catch on mine, she smiles.

"Hey, Lazarus," she says.

Not a nightmare. Naomi would never be in my nightmares.

"Hey…" I shift to sit up in bed. I get a head rush, the world tilting briefly, and I exhale slowly until my vision reorients. "I feel like I did something very dramatic."

"You did. You big drama queen."

She's smiling, but her eyes look sleepless and nervous.

She reaches over and slips her fingers in between mine. Her fingers are usually filled with chunky rings. Right now, they're naked, and her hand seems small compared to mine.

"You scared the shit out of us."

Us. "Where's Diego?"

"He's talking to your dad, I think."

She must mean Donovan. My stomach churns when I think about how my father must be crucifying Diego right now.

Naomi pulls her lips in. "They didn't tell me much, but…it has to do with your kidney, doesn't it?"

I let out a deep breath. *I've been avoiding this conversation for too long.*

"Yes," I confess. "It's my kidney. Look…the truth is, it's been going downhill for a few months now."

Her mouth purses in concern. "Is that…normal?"

I nod. "Yeah. More or less."

"So…why not tell me about it? Did you think I couldn't handle it?"

I hesitate. "No. That's not it. It's…ah. It's just complicated."

She shifts forward. "I'm a smart woman. Try me."

I press my lips in a half-smile. "I know you are. You're the smartest woman I know."

I take those fingers laced in mine and pull them to my lips. I kiss her knuckles and the backs of her hands. Naomi rises and presses her mouth to mine.

She's so soft, so warm, and I want to live in this forever.

But when she pulls back, those brown eyes are glittering. She holds my gaze. "Otto. What aren't you telling me?"

I clear my throat. "I didn't want to tell you…because I knew you'd try to talk me out of it."

"Try to talk you out of…what, exactly?"

"I'm not getting another transplant."

A thick, heavy silence falls between us.

"Otto—"

"I'm not doing it." End. Period. I look her in the eyes

when I say it this time so she knows I'm serious. "I know my rights. I can refuse treatment if I want to."

"Why would you…?"

"I'm not giving up this kidney. I'm not."

"It's a kidney. A failing kidney. Why would you hold on to that?"

"It's mine."

Her jaw sets, confusion and thick frustration in her voice. "If you don't take the transplant, you could die."

"It's my choice."

"What about me? What about my choices? If I lose you—"

"If you lose me, you'll find someone else."

Silence stretches out between us, dark and heavy.

"Was that what last night was?" she asks finally. "The threesome? Were you…*giving* me to Diego?"

My lips thin. "Not giving. Giving implies that I own you. You and Diego are the best people I know. You're good together."

"So, what. You're afraid I can't handle being alone?"

"No. I'm afraid *he* can't be alone. He lost his mother and…"

My voice stoppers in my throat, and I can't bring it back.

She puts her hand on my wrist. "If you don't want him to be alone, then don't *leave*."

I don't say anything. I can't. I want her to give up. I want her to leave me alone.

Naomi isn't finished, though. She presses with "Last night, you told me you loved me. Did you mean it?"

My jaw clenches so tight, I might snap my molars.

"Otto. Did you mean it? Because if you did…that's pretty fucked-up. You can't tell me you love me and then make me watch you die."

"It was a mistake," I snap. "I shouldn't have said that. I'm sorry."

She stares at me. Tears dance in her eyes.

My soul has been sucked straight out from my chest, and there's nothing I can do about it.

I've made my choice. These are the consequences.

I have to break her heart. It's the only way she'll move on.

It's the only way she'll let me go.

"Get fucked, Otto," she says.

She doesn't sound angry, though.

She sounds hurt.

She storms out of the room and out of my life.

13

KENZI

[text: Donovan] Otto is in the hospital
[text: Donovan] Come when you can

That's the text I get that has me sprinting to Lighthouse Medical.

Luckily, I'm not far—I went to the mainland for some last-minute Christmas gifts. I found a sweater Otto's size that I decided would look good on him, but I abandon it with the person at the checkout counter the second I get Donovan's text.

I get in my car, drive to the ferry, and listen to the pounding of my own heartbeat as I wait for the minutes to tick by painfully slowly until the ferry comes back around.

I'm trying not to launch into a full-blown panic.

Otto is in the hospital. My baby boy is sick.

He's been sick his whole life. He was a sick child—so much so that I'd had to strap him into a helmet when we left the house so he wouldn't hurt his head if he fainted.

The kidney transplant helped, but it wasn't a cure-all. He's had to keep up with immunosuppressants, making him extra susceptible to anything and everything. Anything from a minor cold to a rare swine flu; if it's floating around, he'll got it.

I should be used to these kinds of texts. But I'm not.

Every time I get them, it sends a sick rush of adrenaline pumping through my veins. My vision blurs, my heartbeat is loud in my ears, and even though I have the car window cracked open, I'm sweating bullets underneath my puffy winter coat.

Finally, the ferry arrives and carries me and my car across the lake and to Hannsett Island. It's a bright, clear-blue day, and gulls swoop overhead. Every now and then, they perch on the ferry, hop around the ice, and then shake the cold off their wings and take flight again.

The ferry gets closer, bringing the lighthouse into view. It's a tall, red structure that's been around for ages. Attached to the lighthouse are the two main wings of the Lighthouse Medical Center. Donovan runs the Lighthouse Medical Center, Jason operates as a surgeon as needed, and now Otto is there, too.

No matter what, we always circle back to this place.

The ferry pulls in and drops the ramp, letting us out. I chug my car up the main road and into the medical center parking lot.

I'm right behind Jason. He steps out of his cab smartly dressed in a navy blue suit. He must have come fresh out of shooting his promo spot.

"Jason!"

He turns at his name. His expression melts from one of anxiety to relief.

I rush to him, and he wraps his arms around me. He swallows me up in his huge frame. For a minute, I'm safe.

Jason King is the human equivalent of a Snuggie.

"You okay?" he asks.

"I'm terrified," I tell him honestly.

He kisses the top of my head. Then he takes my hand in his and gives a squeeze.

It's his way of saying: *whatever we're walking into, we'll do it together.*

Jason is nothing if not the most loyal man I've ever met.

We walk into the hospital, hand in hand. A couple of doctors who know us stop us briefly to say hi, but their smiles are weak.

It's that feeling of walking into a room when everyone knows something you don't.

The lump of panic is rising in my chest. Jason texts Donovan, who gives us the room number. I take deep breaths as we take the elevator up.

"It's going to be okay," Jason tells me.

I know he's trying to be comforting, but he can't know that.

No one can.

I say nothing and let the elevator carry us.

Donovan is waiting for us outside of Otto's room.

It's the three of us again. The Three Muskrats.

Donovan gives me a tight squeeze, and we break apart. When he spots Jason, however, he just gives the other man a nod and a "Hey."

It's weird. Things have been weird ever since Donovan stopped sleeping in our bed nearly a month ago.

It's not a divorce. Not a break*up*. Just a *break*.

Things had been strained in our household ever since Maria died earlier this year.

As it turns out, both my husbands have completely incompatible ways of dealing with grief. Jason refused to talk about Maria at all. Donovan, meanwhile, woke us up nearly every night thrashing in his sleep.

Donovan had been with her when she'd passed. It was hard on him.

But with one man refusing to acknowledge the elephant

in the room while the elephant was sitting on the other man's chest...well.

It got bad.

All three of us agreed to take some space. Breathe for a second. Come back together after the holidays and figure things out from there.

It killed me to agree to it. I didn't want to spend any period of time away from Donovan. But from the hollowed-out, pained look in his eyes, I knew...

He wasn't requesting space. He was *begging* for space. And if he didn't get it, things were just going to go from bad to worse.

But now, standing here with the two of them and this knife-sharp tension between the three of us, all I can think is: *Dear God, if I only get one Christmas miracle this year, please let these boys get along.*

"How is he?" Jason asks. His voice is clipped, professional.

Jason and Donovan both work at the same hospital. If nothing else, they're good at being in business mode around each other.

Donovan's lips turn downward in a way I've come to know means *bad news*. "It's his kidney."

My breath catches. "Is it time?"

"Yeah. It's time."

"Okay." I slip my hand through my hair. "We've planned for this. We knew this was coming. Maybe not this soon, but...it's going to be okay." I rake my fingers through my hair. "I want to see him."

Donovan steps aside to let me through.

I open the door, and when Otto sees it's me, a lopsided smile cuts across his face.

Even at thirty, my boy is a sweet boy, and he's always happy to see his mama.

But as soon as the smile is there, it vanishes, when he remembers where he is and *why I'm here*.

Why we're all here.

"Hey, baby," I say to him. I press a kiss to the top of his head and sit down on the hospital bed beside him.

"Hey." His smile is weak now. "Sorry. My present kind of sucks this year."

I link my fingers in between his. It's so hard to see him like this.

"What happened?" I ask.

"Did Donovan tell you?"

"Tell us what?"

All eyes turn to Donovan. Donovan clears his throat. "Otto has been hiding his blood work results and using Diego to cover for him. He's been in renal failure for some time now."

My mouth drops open. I look back at my son and ask, "Otto…why?"

"Because I knew if I told you, you'd freak out."

"Okay, well…I'm calm." I force my voice to be level. "I think I'm impressively calm, all things considered. This doesn't have to be a dramatic situation. We'll call your sister and explain what's going on… How long is the flight from London? Seven hours?"

"No." Otto says it so quietly, I almost don't hear him.

"No?"

"*No*." Now his voice is firm. Those blue eyes fix on mine. "I'm not getting a new kidney."

I look at Donovan, my mouth open. He just crosses his arms over his chest in a half shrug.

Jason comes over and puts his hand on Otto's shoulder. "Look, buddy, I just want you to understand…at this stage, the organ is in complete failure. We can't revive it."

"Don't talk to me like a kid." Otto's eyes flash. "I know how this works. I'm an adult. I get to make my own choices about my body."

"Okay." I smooth my hand over Otto's. "So what do *you* want to do?"

Instead of answering, he turns to look at Donovan.

He's always looked to Donovan for answers.

Donovan takes his cue. "Nixing the organ transplant, we can get you on some infusions to flush your kidney. Then it's a rigorous schedule of dialysis treatments."

"Yeah," Otto says. "We'll do that."

Otto leans his head back against the headboard and closes his eyes. He looks weary. Tired.

It sends pinpricks straight through my heart.

It feels like just yesterday we were here. Twenty years ago, Otto and I traveled from England to the small island of Hannsett to get help when Otto became incredibly sick. It was that same trip that he met his biological father, Jason, for the first time. While they were treating him, I fell back in love with both Jason and Donovan. When we found out that Otto needed a new kidney, I didn't know how I'd get through it. Jason and I weren't able to donate. Donovan was. Donovan gave Otto the kidney he needed, and the rest is history.

I knew it wouldn't last forever. But I didn't need forever —I just needed more time.

And now we're back to square one. Back at the place I never wanted to be.

Otto has a match. His little sister, Joan. Joan is eighteen now. She's always wanted to be there for her older brother— even if that means making the incredible choice of a kidney donation.

But never in a million years did I imagine Otto would say *no*.

Jason stands. He moves to the door and gives Donovan's shoulder a pat. As he exits, I hear him murmur to the other man, "Let's talk."

"Yep."

Donovan's brown eyes meet my gaze briefly, and then he turns and heads outside with Jason.

I notice their locked jaws, tensed postures.

I look back at Otto. He looks half-asleep. "Hey, baby...can I get you anything?"

"An extra blanket, maybe?" he asks. He shivers. "It's freezing."

"You've got it."

I stand, kiss the top of his head, and make my way to the door.

"Mom." I stop and glance back at him. He smiles weakly. "Thanks."

I know what he's saying. *Thanks for not pushing me on this.*

He has no idea how hard it is to keep myself from shaking him by the shoulders and screaming, *I'm your mom! Say yes to the kidney! Do what I tell you to do!*

But he's a grown man now. And I have to let that part of me go.

So I just smile back at him. "You're my bacon."

"You're mine."

It's our way of saying *I love you*. It's been our secret code, ever since he was a kid.

With that, I exit his room. Immediately, I walk into chaos.

"*—all your fault!*"

Great. *Here we go.*

I exhale and see Jason jabbing his finger into Donovan's chest. Donovan barks a bitter, scathing laugh. "*My* fault?"

"He's holding on to that kidney because it's *yours*! You need to go in there and tell him to let go!"

"Right, because you know what's best for everyone, don't you?" Donovan's smile is sharp. "Dr. King. Fucking guru of medicine. We're just lucky to kiss your ass—"

"Stop it!"

At the sound of my voice, both men turn to me and swallow their tongues.

"It's Christmas Eve." I seethe. "It's goddamn, fucking Christmas Eve, and I'm spending it in the hospital while our son goes into organ failure. Now I have to deal with the two of you arguing like children on top of it."

"Sorry," Jason says quickly.

Donovan stays silent. He just stares at the floor, jaw tight, arms crossed over his chest.

I sigh. "Work this out. Or don't. I don't care. But he needs us right now." I look at Donovan and add pointedly, "All three of us. United."

14

DIEGO

I'm getting fired.

That's it. I'm definitely getting fired.

Dr. Donovan hasn't said as much, but I know it. There's no way to come back from this.

He pulled me aside, and I told him everything. I told him about when I first noticed Otto's toxin levels rising in September. I told him about how Otto had begged me to keep it a secret—*I need my friend Diego*, he'd told me, *not Doctor Diego*.

So I did. I kept his secret. I kept his results away from prying eyes. I pretended like everything was normal.

I sat on my hands, and I did nothing as Otto got worse and worse.

This is on me. My fault.

I feel like I've swallowed a tennis ball.

There's no coming back from this. His son is sick. His son is dying. And I prioritized my friendship instead of my patient's needs.

I'll be fired. Probably kicked out of the medical field completely.

And now, there's nothing to do but sit here and swallow back my shame and guilt.

There's a chair in the hall. I take it. I close my eyes and rest my head on the wall. My head is throbbing, a purpling headache.

"Diego?"

I glance up. Helen Humphrey is calling me over.

She has her gray sweater pulled over her hands, and she twists the fabric anxiously as she approaches.

Immediately, I stand up. I do my best to push all thoughts of Otto to the back of my mind. "Mrs. Humphrey. Is everything okay?"

When we got the results of the CT scan yesterday, I didn't find anything abnormal in his scans, so I discharged him. It didn't seem right to keep him in the hospital for Christmas Eve when nothing was technically wrong.

"He fainted again. This morning."

My heart falls. *Crap*. What did I miss…?

"I wanted to see if you had the results of those blood tests—"

"Sorry," I say quickly. "We've been busy today."

I'm in plain clothes. I'm technically off the clock. But—

"I'll go check on him right now," I tell her.

"Diego." Her voice is tight suddenly. "I…well. There's something I feel like I should tell you."

My skin tingles. *Here we go…*

"You can tell me anything," I tell her.

Helen glances away and lets out a huff of a sigh. "He's just…he's been such a curmudgeon. I was tired of it, you know? I just wanted one nice, happy holiday season."

"Alright…"

"And then I saw those commercials on TV. The ones for that pill Promext."

I fight back a wince. Promext is yet another "miracle

drug" they've been advertising around. It calls itself an antidepressant, but it's recently been recalled for—

Oh. Suddenly. I see where this is going.

"I know I shouldn't have," she says in a rush. "But I thought, what could it hurt? I started crushing up the pills and putting them in his coffee. For a couple days, he was happy! Really happy! I didn't think it would—"

I give her arm a squeeze. "Thank you for telling me. Which room is he in?"

"402." There's alarm in her voice now. "Did I do something wrong…?"

"Stay here."

"Doctor—"

I don't have time to finish my explanation. I take off down the hall. When I rush into Mr. Humphrey's room, I see it's already a flurry of activity.

"What happened?" I ask.

Two nurses and a doctor crowd around Mr. Humphrey. He has an oxygen mask on, and his eyes are rolling back.

"Who are you?" the doctor says, annoyed.

Dr. Donovan charged me with this patient. He's my responsibility.

"I'm his doctor."

The doctor's eyes flicker over me briefly. "He's coding," the doctor tells me, his voice short and impatient. He starts to tell me the list of medications he's giving him, but immediately, I interrupt.

"Don't. He's on Promext. It's a hemorrhagic stroke." I step in, calling the orders. The nurses glance at me, then at the doctor. "*Now*," I tell them.

The nurses follow my instructions, getting to work. His blood pressure levels out, and the rapid bleating of the heart rate machine diminishes.

The red numbers flicker to green. He's level again.

One of the nurses looks up at me and gives me a small smile. "Good work, Doctor."

I realize I've broken into a sweat. My legs are suddenly jelly, and I have to brace myself against the wall.

Mr. Humphrey could have died on me. We were *this close*.

He's okay. He's going to be okay.

I close my eyes, and for just a moment, I let myself breathe a sigh of relief.

15

DONOVAN

What a goddamn fucking day.

I leave Kenzi and Jason and escape into my office. There are windows in here. Lots of them. Big windows, overlooking the lighthouse where the hospital got its namesake.

It used to be Jason's dad's old office. Now it's mine, with the words DR. ADAM DONOVAN, CEO on a placard on my desk. My flag in the ground.

I close the door behind me and thumb open the top button on my shirt. I can breathe better now. Outside, the sunset rips claw marks of red and orange into the sky.

I'm not alone for long.

I hear my door open, then click shut again. I know him so annoyingly well—the way his footsteps have purpose, the way he overcompensates for his strong and long limbs by extra-gingerly closing doors—that I don't even have to turn around to know who it is.

"What do you want?" I say, unable to keep the exasperation out of my tone.

"I want to apologize," Jason says. "I lost my temper earlier. I didn't mean to blow up at you."

I turn around to face him and lean into my desk. I touch my fingertips to the wood, poised there.

Jason is an enormously tall man. Six five. Lean. His crisp blue shirt is popped open at the top, the V exposing a strong clavicle underneath a throat equipped with a protruding Adam's apple and a sharp jawline. Age has only run its fingers through his hair, silvering the raven black from the edges in.

He looks so fucking heterosexual right now. I want to tell him that. I want to hurt him. I don't know why.

"Bullshit," I say evenly.

He blinks those big, dumb blues. "What's bullshit?"

"Yes, you did lose your temper. And yes, you did mean to blow up at me."

The divot at the corners of his mouth deepens. "It wasn't fair to you."

"Our son is killing himself with my kidney. Nothing about this is fair."

Jason's lips part. "I'm just saying—"

"Say it."

"I'm sorry."

"That's it?"

Again, he frowns. "Yeah. That's it."

"Great. What do you want from me?"

"Nothing. I just wanted you to hear it, I guess."

"Read and received. You can sleep well tonight."

The noise that leaves Jason's throat isn't quite a sigh, but it's close. "You're clearly not in the mood to talk," he reasons. "So I'm going to go."

"Probably a good idea."

Jason is glass. Smooth and unrippled.

I'm thorns. I'm full of thorns. And if he doesn't leave soon, I'll skewer us both.

He turns to leave, but then my tongue betrays me.

"I miss when you were an asshole," I tell him.

He stops in his tracks. Those frosted blue eyes stare. "No. You don't."

"Go ahead. I know you want to. Hit me. Push me against the wall. Call me a coward. That's what you want to do, isn't it? You may have everyone else fooled, but I think your good-boy act is bullshit. Stop holding back."

Jason's blue eyes flash. For a second, there it is—that angry, poisonous boy he used to be. "You want me to stop holding back?"

My tongue momentarily sticks to the roof of my mouth. The logical part of my brain is already regretting this.

But the touch-starved masochist in me answers: "*Yes.*"

The word barely leaves my lips before Jason closes the distance between us and slams his mouth against mine.

I part my lips and taste him. The heady wood-earth scent of his cologne. Cool mint on his tongue. That pent-up longing that comes on too hard and leaves my lips feeling swollen and bruised.

I'm sure I taste like my umpteenth cup of coffee and desperation, but *I don't care*. I grab at his shirt and rip at it. Buttons plink against my desk and fall to the floor. His shirt hangs open, and I run my hands over his hard body. His skin is burning hot. I lick his jaw. I bite his throat. The moan he makes is fucking animal, so I kiss him again just to feel it vibrate against my lips.

"Lock the door," I tell him.

He smiles against my mouth. "No."

"*No?*"

"No. I want everyone to know you're my bitch."

That shouldn't make all my blood rush to my cock, but it does. He cups my groin, and I lean against the desk, spreading to give him better access. His hands are huge, corded with veins, and he rubs my erection through my pants.

I'm swollen, needy, and those fingers know me too well.

Even his fumbling caresses over the fabric make me leak. It's the confidence for me—the way he grips and squeezes with just enough pressure to make my mouth go dry.

I paw at his belt. I want to tear his clothes from his body. As I pull at his clothes, my mouth devours his skin.

I lick and bite his chest. His tight nipples. His hairy armpits.

I'm fucking feral.

Jason is like me. His touches are rough and hungry. He grips me, his fingers tight, as though I'll float away at any second if he doesn't keep a firm hold on me.

We grab at each other so desperately that, eventually, we both lose our balance. I fall to the floor with a grunt. Jason is on top of me. He takes advantage of the position and closes his hands around my wrists. He pins them to the gray carpet above my head. Now, I'm panting, spread out and vulnerable underneath him.

Those blue eyes glitter down at me.

He says, "You're an animal, you know that?"

"What kind of animal?"

He thinks about it. "A puppy."

I growl. He grins.

"Show me your tongue, puppy."

I do. I open my mouth wide and extend my tongue like I'm at the dentist's.

Jason bows and licks his tongue across mine. The sensation is bizarre, erotic, and makes me whimper.

Then he reaches between us, and I feel him shift from side to side to shimmy his pants and briefs down his legs.

"Keep your tongue out," he says, his voice low and controlled.

Knowing what's coming next, it's hard to keep myself from drooling.

Jason positions himself so he's straddling my chest, his knees under my armpits. His stiff cock stands proudly before me, heavy balls hanging beneath it. Jason King is the dictionary definition of *all man*. With one hand, he fists my hair, and with the other, he fists his cock.

"Keep still."

I don't move—*I barely blink*. I lie there, frozen in place, tongue stretched out achingly far. He slides the head of his cock against my tongue. I taste the velvet of his skin. I taste the salt of his arousal. His breath hitches as he teases himself on my tongue, taking his sweet time.

I'm throbbing in my pants. It's taking everything in me not to swallow him down, but I love this. I love the concentrated look on his face. I love the way he uses my mouth... exactly how he wants it.

"That's it. Now suck."

I unlock my mouth and wrap my lips around him.

He pushes it in deep. My eyes water. My nose stings. I swallow back my gag reflex. I want more.

"Good," Jason says, because Jason loves praise. "Really good."

He releases his grip on my hair and puts his hands on the carpet instead for balance. Now free to move around, I lean forward and greedily suck him, swallowing, licking, tightening my throat around him.

His hips thrust forward, jerkily humping my face, and I moan into it. I grab his tight ass, pulling him into me.

"Oh, fuck," Jason moans, his eyebrows knitting, jaw clenched in agonizing pleasure.

And now he's mine.

I pop him out of my mouth and gasp. I need to catch my breath. He's glistening, beet red, veins plump and angry.

"You did miss me, didn't you?" I ask and wet my lips. They feel raw and swollen.

He looks down at me in a daze, those blues half-lidded.

I shift, perching on my elbow. Then I suck my finger into my mouth to get it wet. I give him a few languid strokes, loving the way he pulses in my hand when I squeeze him tight. Then I slip my hand underneath him, fondling his balls before finding his tight hole. I ease my finger inside of him, loving his tight heat, and press small, teasing kisses from the base of his cock to the tip as I enter him.

"*Jesusfuck*," Jason moans. One word. His hips rut forward instinctively, hunting for more, but I keep him wanting.

"Quiet," I remind him.

A nurse is going to think someone is *dying* in here.

But that doesn't stop me from tormenting him further.

I trace the tip of my tongue over those veins, mapping him.

This is the game we play. He pins me to the ground. Degrades me. Makes me want.

And then I make him beg.

I swallow him down, finally, when I decide he's had enough teasing. With my finger buried inside of him, caressing, it doesn't take long to push him to his edge.

It's that little noise he makes that tips me off. Mouth shut tight, eyebrows furrowed, he hums on a small *mm*. The sound of someone biting their tongue.

Before he blows in my mouth, I release him from my lips. I pant. I give his cock sweet kisses. Tiny licks. I wait until he stops twitching, until those blue eyes are looking back down at me expectantly. Only then do I swallow him again, sucking.

I repeat this three more times, bringing him right to the edge, only to pull back at the last second. Each time I start again, he gets there quicker. The last time I pull back, he curses, thrusts forward. His abdomen is clenched tight, and his thighs are shaking around me.

"Breathe," I tell him.

He gulps in air. His face is bright pink.

His hands are fists, pressed against the carpeted floor like a runner about to take off. His knuckles have gone white.

"What're you doing to me?" He groans.

I look him directly in the eyes and give him a slow, long lick that sends a full-body shudder through him. "I want you to explode the second you push inside of me."

His eyes flicker. It's his *I'm done with your games* look.

He puts his hand on my chest and forces me back down to the floor so quickly, it knocks the breath out of me. A breath that he swallows as his lips capture mine.

"Need you," he mumbles. Not *I need you*, not *I need to fuck you*, just *need you*, because I've teased him so relentlessly that his brain has detached from his spinal cord and he's doing the best he can.

He yanks my pants down and spits in his palm. The anticipation of what comes next sends a shiver through me. I try to swallow, but my arousal is like a dry pill in my throat. Then I feel him, his hand cupping my ass, a finger pressing inside of me, then a second finger. I've been so focused on his pleasure, I haven't thought about mine, and the second he starts to fondle me, I feel like I've bitten into a live wire. Electric heat zips through me, and I gasp, pressing back into his hand, needing more.

Jason slots himself between my legs, and then I feel him, the thick head of him.

It doesn't take one thrust. It takes three. Three before he moans, and I know he can't hold back anymore. I push my hips upward and rut against him, my dripping cock rubbing against his hard stomach. We move as one, gripping each other, and I rip my nails into his back. I bite his shoulder, his neck. He fills me so completely, so fully, and the stretch aches so good.

"*Donovan*," he swears as he gives a final thrust and spills over inside of me.

His release unravels me. I moan into the crook of his neck and shudder underneath him. My pleasure explodes, spilling over my belly and splashing onto his. We're wet with it, sticky.

I came so hard, my mouth tastes like metal. I'm panting, blinking at the ceiling. It takes me a long second to remember that I'm at the Lighthouse Medical Center, in my very own office, and I should probably put on some clothes.

"Fuck," Jason says. He pulls out of me, and the absence of him makes my whole body buzz. He sits up and awkwardly works on pulling his pants over his hips. "I needed that."

"Yeah. Me too."

Now, when we're not grabbing each other and tearing at skin, it's harder to talk to each other again. We've cleaved apart—literally and figuratively.

I sit up. My pants are around my ankles, and I pull them up over my hips.

"Come back home," Jason says suddenly. Unprompted.

I look up at him and narrow my eyes. "What, and keep the two of you awake?"

"Are you still having nightmares of her?"

"Maria. You can say her name, can't you?"

The edge of Jason's mouth pushes downward.

"Or was she just a glorified nanny to you?"

"You don't really think that."

"I don't know what to think. Because you won't fucking *talk* about it."

"I was afraid of losing you."

I squint at him. "What? You thought I would...what, try to fuck my grief out with other people? I'd never be unfaithful to you two."

"No. Not like that." Jason has a tic, and he's doing it now. He fiddles with the two wedding rings around his finger. When he's uncomfortable or trying to distract himself, he twists them around and around in circles, like a fidget spinner. It's like watching Linus suck on his comfort blanket. "I was afraid of losing you to your sadness. When you get depressed…it's like a living thing. It swallows you whole."

He's not exactly wrong about that. I encircle my hand around my wrist and find myself unconsciously rubbing my thumb at the leather bracelet there.

I've let myself drown in my misery in the past. Self-harm. Self-hatred. Jason knows better than anyone how dangerous my grief can be.

As much as I don't want it to, as much as I'd rather hold on to my anger, his words roll away some of the stones on my chest. Still— "I didn't need you to save me," I tell him. He *needs* to hear this if we're ever going to find a way forward. "And I didn't need you to dive into the depths with me. I just needed you to let me sink and be there for me when I was ready to swim back up."

Those eyes meet mine. This is the most candid we've been with each other in months—hell, maybe *years*. I see a flicker of recognition finally settle into those blue orbs.

"I'm here," he says firmly. "I'm not going anywhere. Ever."

I bite my lip. "Yeah. I know."

"Are you ready now?"

"Ready for what?"

"To swim back up?"

I glance away. "I don't know."

"Okay," he says. Not disappointed. Not guilt-tripping me. Just…*okay*.

An awkward silence settles between us.

"Do you think I should talk to Otto?" I ask.

Change of topic. It'll do us both good.

"He worships you." And then those blue eyes meet mine. So goddamn earnest. "We all do."

Words stick in the back of my throat.

Words like *I miss waking up to your dumb face every morning*.

But pride is a bitch.

Jason gets up off the floor. He finishes getting dressed. As he untucked his cuffs, he adds, "I need to go pick up some things for Otto. I should get going."

"Hey."

He goes to the door. He puts his hand on the handle but then stops. He turns and looks at me.

Those are the eyes of the boy who tormented me through our teenage years.

The man who claimed me in front of his parents, even though he knew they'd crucify him for it.

The surgeon who held my hand before cutting me open on his operating table.

My Jason. The same person who slipped a ring on my finger under a canopy of stars and promised to love me and care for me for the rest of our lives.

Isn't that what he's doing now? Just trying to love me.

Yet every time he reaches his hand out for me, I bite it.

Why am I like this?

I purse my lips.

"I have a favor to ask," I tell him. Then I get to my feet and reach for the desk to grab Humphrey's copy of Jason's book.

16

OTTO

Mom was generous enough to lend me her headphones so I can listen to music or watch movies on my phone. Which is good, because I need the distraction.

Dialysis is a pain in the…well. *Kidneys*.

My mom rolled me in a wheelchair down the hall to the infusion room. I'm one person in a row of twenty getting infusions. I sit in a thick, plush chair as the dialysis machine whirrs and churns beside me.

Bad blood out, good blood in.

I can feel my kidney. It's not something you should be able to feel, but I can feel it—the outline of the thing, a poisonous, heavy sac in my side. It feels swollen and tender, and I imagine it like a bruise, purple and ugly.

I cup my hand against my side the way a mother might hold her unborn child. Except the thing I'm pregnant with is actively trying to kill me.

The sound of a chair scraping across the floor wakes me up. I quickly pull my hand away from my side, as though I've been caught in the act.

But it's just Donovan. He's pulled up a chair and sits

across from me. He leans forward, lacing his fingers together.

I pluck out my headphones. "Hey."

"Hey. Thought I'd check in. See how you're doing."

I glance down the room. Most of the chairs are empty—no one wants to go through treatment on Christmas Eve. There are two other people in here besides me, an older man who has fallen asleep in his chair and a woman with her head in her phone.

"I feel like I'm on the set of *The Walking Dead*."

Donovan's mouth pinches in a wry half-smile.

"Otherwise?" I continue. "I'm great."

My body disagrees with a throbbing pinch that twists in my gut. I've broken out in a fever sweat that collects at my forehead and under my pits. I wipe at my hairline, trying to ignore it.

"I talked to your sister," Donovan says. "She's on the plane."

My jaw sets. "Tell her she's wasting her time."

Donovan folds one leg over the other. He nods toward my phone.

"What're you watching?"

I turn the screen toward him so he can see.

"*Dr. Who?*"

I nod. "Yep. It's my comfort show."

"Number Four. Classic. My favorite Doctor."

"Yeah. I know." I chance a glance at Donovan. He's staring down at the screen in my lap, watching the episode play out. I hesitate, then say, "Do you remember Camp-Outs?"

A small smile curls Donovan's mouth. "How could I forget?"

My voice is forceful, a train barreling through this conversation. "Every Friday night, we'd blow up the mattress in the living room. One of the adults would stay with me, and we'd watch movies, eat s'mores, and pass out on the mattress. It didn't even matter when Joan was born, because by the time she was old enough to pick movies for Camp-Outs, I was *too old* for them.

"Mom always made them fun. Jason always let me watch whatever I wanted to watch and eat as many cookies as I wanted to eat. But with you, it was like…every time, you came in with a purpose. You always had some bizarre, 1970s sci-fi movie that no one else had ever heard about, and you were so eager to share it with me. Like your entire life, you'd been waiting for someone to sit down and watch *Forbidden Planet* with you. And then afterwards, when the movie was over, you'd let me talk—and I could talk about anything. You'd listen. You wouldn't offer advice or tell me how to feel or what to do. You'd just listen.

"I always tried to stay awake on your nights. I never wanted them to end." I shake my head. "Of course, years later, I realized it wasn't exactly *special Otto time* but more like…special date-night time. It was your way of giving each other space."

Donovan presses his lips together. "It was both," he says. "Two of us had date night. The other had Otto-time. Both were special."

I let out a breath. "Maybe I should've given you more time with them. Less time with me."

Donovan blinks at me. "What makes you say that?"

"Can we be transparent right now? Can we just be two people who are completely transparent? No bullshit."

Donovan nods. "Alright. No bullshit."

"Are you breaking up with mom and Jason?"

Donovan looks down.

"No," he says. His voice is low, firm. "What we're going through right now…it's hard. Yes. But we're not splitting. And even if we did…I'd never leave you. You know that, don't you?"

"Why not? You don't have anything tethering yourself to me."

Donovan stares at me, and there's genuine shock on his face. "Otto, that's not true—"

I stay quiet at that. I don't know if I can get any more words out without bursting into tears, so I hold them all in. I hold everything in.

The doctors used to call me *such a strong boy. Such a brave boy*.

Such a numb boy. That's what I really was.

So-fucking-good-at-repressing-everything boy.

But I guess that didn't fit as neatly on a Get-Well card.

Donovan is relentless, though. He presses the point home with "No matter what happens…I'm not going to leave you. That's a promise."

I suck in a breath. I have my strength again. My numbness.

"I'm tired," I say. "I think I'd like to be alone now."

Donovan hesitates, but he knows better. My walls are up now, and there's no scaling them.

"I'll come back later," he says. He gets up, then rakes his fingers through my hair affectionately and adds, "Love you, buddy."

Then he's gone. I can't move. I can't breathe. If I do, I might break down.

So I stay completely still and completely numb. I shove my headphones in my ears, turn the volume up all the way, and let the seconds tick by, painfully aware that every second that passes, I'm getting weaker.

17

DIEGO

*A*t 6:00 p.m., I discharge Mr. Humphrey.

I linger in the hallway for a minute. I've left the door to their room open, and through it, I can see the Humphreys try to navigate their way out. Helen tries to help Hugo get his socks on, but he snaps at her when she gets them on the wrong foot.

Didn't even know that was a thing.

"The Grinch is back."

I turn my head and see Dr. Donovan come up next to me. He leans against the wall, his arms folded across his chest.

He's out of his lab coat, and he has a leather satchel hanging off his side. He's on his way out.

I nod. "Thank god for that."

"I'd rather thank you. Sum it up for me."

I give him the full story. I tell him about Helen's confession and how that led to my diagnosis. I tell him about how we were able to stabilize Hugo. I tell him the list of medications I prescribed Hugo, as well as the therapist I encouraged him to reach out to so he can get stabilized with the correct medications.

"Sounds like the truth saved his life," Dr. Donovan says.

"Yeah. It did." My mind drifts. Otto. Naomi. All the truths I've kicked under the rug.

"Nurse Kadish said you did great," Dr. Donovan tells me.

A twinge of pride in my chest. I try to keep it off my face. "I was just doing my job." I glance up at him nervously and address the elephant in the room. "If…I still have a job, that is."

Donovan looks back at me, and I can feel his stare.

"I'd say the hospital needs more men like you, not less."

"But—"

"You lied to protect Otto. Don't do it again. This is your only warning."

Relief floods my chest. "Yes, sir."

Donovan looks tired. He pulls at the collar of his shirt, loosening it.

"It's late," he says. "And you weren't even supposed to be working today. Go home."

"Otto—"

"He'll stay here tonight. We'll see how he's doing tomorrow."

Christmas Eve at the hospital. I know it's not what Otto wanted.

But there's not a lot we can do about that now.

Donovan's expression softens. "Get some rest, Diego."

He starts to leave but then stops. "Oh. Before I forget." He reaches into his bag. He pulls out Humphrey's copy of Jason's book. He holds it out to me. "Jason signed it."

I take the book. "Thanks. He'll like this."

Donovan puts his hand on my shoulder and gives it a squeeze.

The gesture is familial, affectionate, and it means more than he knows.

"Dr. Donovan," I say as he starts to leave. He glances back at me, his eyebrows lifted. "Merry Christmas."

A smile enters his eyes, even if it doesn't quite make it to his mouth. "Merry Christmas, Diego."

* * *

I have one stop to make before I go home.

The door is open to Otto's room, but I knock before entering anyway.

He tears his eyes away from his phone and looks up at me. His eyes are bright. That easy, boyish smile crosses his lips.

It's easy to believe he's going to be okay when I see him like this.

Unfortunately, I know too well the hell his body is going through right now.

"I was wondering when you'd show your face," Otto says.

I motion inside. "Can I come in?"

"Make yourself at home."

I come in and sit down on the edge of the bed beside him. For a minute, neither of us says anything. It just feels good to sit beside my friend.

Then Otto sighs. "Hell of a way to spend Christmas, huh?"

"At least you had Hanukkah."

There's that crooked grin. "There is that."

Silence normally isn't uncomfortable between us. We lean into it. But right now, the air around us feels tense. Static.

"Say it," Otto says finally.

"What?"

"Tell me I'm crazy. I can hear you thinking it. You have a terrible poker face. Never go to Vegas—they'll eat you alive."

I shake my head. "I don't think you're crazy."

"Well, then you're the only one. I already got the lecture from Naomi. And Donovan. And my mom."

"Not Jason?"

"He's too busy running around making sure everyone else doesn't fall to pieces to lecture me."

"I'm not here to lecture you." I look up at him, straight in the eyes, so he knows I mean it. "I'm just here to listen."

At that, there's a shift in Otto's expression. The angry, defensive lines on his face are replaced with something softer.

He opens up.

"Jason is my dad. Biologically. Whatever. I don't want to downplay it—he didn't have to be in my life, but he was. He stepped up. Hell, he stepped *over and beyond*."

"I know you love him," I reassure him.

"Yeah. It's just…growing up, Jason was my dad, but Donovan, he was…" His voice falters. He swallows. Tries again, this time with strength behind his words. "He was my hero. He gave me a new life. Literally. I can't explain it."

"You can to me."

Otto presses his lips tightly together. "It's like I lived two lifetimes. Before this kidney. After this kidney. I was born twice. I don't…" Words stop and start again. "I don't know who I am without him."

"Don't you mean without *it*?"

Otto glances at me. "Both."

A small silence settles between us. I pick my next words carefully. "The people you love…they're always with you. Always. I don't know what's going to happen with your parents. I don't know if they'll work things out or not. But I do know that we all have to outlive them eventually. You, Otto, are a bright, brilliant soul. With or without Donovan. That's all you."

"I don't feel so bright or brilliant right now."

He stares off at the wall, but his eyes look vacant. Empty.

I can't hold it back anymore. My chest is buzzing, and my throat is tight, and I can't bite my tongue anymore. It comes spilling out. The truth. "I love you," I blurt out.

Otto looks at me. There's life in his eyes again. Not the shell-of-Otto. *Otto.* Those brilliant, vibrant eyes. He watches me with a mixture of confusion and curiosity dancing in his expression.

I continue. "And before you say that I'll move on, I'll find someone else…I don't think I will. I know you don't believe in soul mates, but my mom believed in them, and so do I. Whatever we are—friends, lovers, something that they don't even have a word for yet—I don't know. I *do* know that we're soul mates. And you only get one of those in your lifetime.

"So if I lost you, yeah. I'd grieve. I'd survive. I've lost people I've loved before, and I made it through it. I'll find family again. People I care about. But I'm never, ever going to find another soul mate. That's a fact."

Otto shifts in his spot. There's a pained look on his face, his eyes half-squinted. "Diego—"

"Don't apologize," I interrupt him. "Don't say things you don't mean or try to soothe me. I'm not saying this to guilt you. I just…felt like you should know."

Otto stares at me for a long moment. Then he nods and says, simply, "Okay. Thank you for telling me."

I exhale a breath I didn't realize I'd been holding.

I don't need to hear him say those words back. I don't want him to say it—not now.

It just feels good to get these things off my chest, finally. I feel like I've stepped off a rickety plank of wood I've been balancing on for years and, at last, my feet are on solid ground.

"I'll come by tomorrow," I say. "See how you're doing. Need anything else before I go?"

"No. Thanks."

I rise from my seat. I go to the door, but before I can exit—

"Diego."

I turn. I can tell there's something on the tip of his

tongue. He's wrestling with his words. Finally, he just says, "I'm lucky to have you in my life."

That does draw a small smile from me.

"Get some rest," I tell him. Then I open the door and leave him for the night.

18

NAOMI

It's freezing as I wait for the ferry.

Most people are in their cars. There is a small, heated waiting station for travelers without vehicles, but I don't feel like being crammed inside with strangers.

So I hug myself, tuck my gloved hands under my armpits, and wait in the cold.

I hear a car honk behind me. I ignore it.

I'm used to ignoring people who honk at me.

Then I hear it—"Naomi!"

The voice is familiar, so I glance over my shoulder.

Snow drifts in front of the headlights of a black Mercedes. Jason is in the driver's seat, the passenger window open. He gestures for me, and I approach.

"Hi." I wonder if he can see my streaked makeup in the low light.

"Waiting on the ferry?" he asks.

"Yeah."

He glances at the clock on his phone. "It won't come around for another ten. Want to get out of the cold?"

"Sure. Thanks."

I step into his passenger seat and close the door behind

me. I rub my hands together near the open vent, and a tingling warmth rushes through my fingers.

"You really don't have to wait around with me," I tell him.

He shrugs. "I don't mind."

He's wearing a dark peacoat and suede gloves. The radio is playing lowly, and his fingers tap on the steering wheel in time.

There are bags in the back seat that look stuffed with clothes.

"Is that Otto's?" I ask.

He glances at the back seat, then nods. "Yeah. Some of Kenzi's stuff, too. He's probably going to spend a day or two at the hospital, at least, so I wanted him to have a change of clothes. Brought some books. Something to keep him entertained."

"That's nice of you."

He gives me a sad grin. "It's as much for me as it is for him. It helps me to do something. Keep busy. Otherwise…"

"Otherwise it becomes real?"

"Something like that."

I glance out the window. It's dark outside, but holiday string lights hang from the lanterns, illuminating the road. The lights on the poles are twisted up in holiday forms. Twinkling angels. Colored Christmas trees.

"Does he hate me?" I ask. My voice is nearly a whisper.

"Otto? No. He couldn't."

"It's not…it's not that I don't care."

Out of the edge of my vision, I see Jason nod. "Alright."

But there's an itch rising in me. I need him to understand. I turn to him and insist, "I do care. I love him so much. I had dreams…so many dreams. And now it feels like they've been ripped right out from underneath me. It's like, every time I try to get close to him, he just—"

"Pushes you away," Jason finishes for me. He stares out the window, his gaze far away.

"Yeah," I say. "Exactly."

He blinks, then looks at me, refocusing. Those blue eyes are calm. Listening. "You said you had dreams. What'd they look like?"

"I saw myself with him. I saw us getting an apartment together. Having kids together. Growing old together. It wouldn't be conventional, but it would be *us*. Whatever future we wanted, I just knew we could make it together." I let out a deep sigh. "What an idiot I am, right?"

"You're not an idiot," Jason says firmly.

A car passes us, and the headlights briefly illuminate Jason in the darkness. He looks so much like Otto. Otto in twenty years.

Otto with silver-gray in his hair. Otto with laugh lines around his eyes.

Otto with those same, bright blue eyes but now tinged with experience.

The thought that I might never see Otto this old is paralyzing.

Before I know what I'm doing, I lean over and clumsily push my mouth against Jason's.

My lips barely graze his before he takes me by the shoulders and firmly holds me back. "Whoa, there," he says gently, stalling me like a wild horse.

Immediately, I come back into my body. It's not Otto in the car with me.

My boyfriend's father. I'm kissing my boyfriend's father.

"Shit," I say, putting my hand to my mouth. "Oh my god. I'm so sorry."

"Emotions are…high. I get it."

"I'm sorry."

Jason nods and drops his eyes to the steering wheel.

I want to crawl underneath the tires and let him run me over. I close my eyes.

Dear Lord, make me an ant. Then crush me.

Jason breaks the silence suddenly, and his voice is controlled, firm. "Loving someone...it's not always easy. It's a choice. I could've decided to love only Kenzi. Or only Donovan. Or I could've run away to volunteer in some third-world country and left both of them behind. Instead, every day, I wake up and I make the deliberate choice to love both Kenzi and Donovan. Even when it's hard. *Especially* when it's hard. I gave up my family to love them. And they gave up a lot to love me. Everyone made sacrifices. And I'd do it again for them. A thousand times over.

"Love has to be more than...passion and dreams. It's intentional."

I push my fingers against the air vent, turning the vents one way, then the other. I let Jason's words settle over me like snow.

He continues. "I guess what I'm saying is...whatever decision you make, just make sure it's the right choice for you."

The ferry blares its horn. It's docked.

"You should run if you're going to catch it," Jason says. "They don't wait around. I learned that one the hard way."

"Thanks for the heater."

"Sure."

I get up and exit the car. Before I can get very far, I hear Jason call my name. When I turn back, he's rummaging around in the back seat. He finds a scarf and holds it out the window for me.

"Here," he says.

I shake my head. "Oh, no. I can't."

I've taken enough. His son. His time. His patience.

But Jason keeps holding it out. "Otto will kill me if you freeze to death."

I press my lips together and take the scarf. "Thank you."

He gives a nod, like it's nothing. As I start back toward the ferry, I wind the scarf around my neck. It's cozy and warm, and I inhale.

It smells like pine needles. Like tea leaves.

It smells like *Otto*.

My heart twists in my chest. It's so painful, I suck in a quick breath, and my feet come to a halt. I close my eyes to catch my bearings, and I see:

Otto, bare feet on my coffee table, nibbling on the end of his pen as he stares at his notepad.

Otto, twisted up in my bedsheets, his hand in my panties, his voice in my ear, murmuring as he teases me.

Otto, looking at me with those endlessly blue eyes as he tells me he loves me.

It's a punch in the chest. I'm dizzy with longing for him. A deep, soul-longing.

I open my eyes and gasp in a breath of cold, salty air.

I can't board this ferry.

I turn. Jason hasn't left yet. He's texting in his parking spot, the phone light glowing on his face.

I knock on the window. He lifts his eyes from the screen and rolls the window down.

"Hi." I smile awkwardly. "Sorry. So sorry. Can you drive me somewhere? I'll keep my hands to myself this time. I promise."

The edges of his eyes crinkle with a small smile. "Hop in."

19

DIEGO

I'm home when my phone buzzes.

I'm nursing two fingers of whiskey, but I set it down on my coaster to check it.

[text: Naomi] You up?

I glance at my watch. It's almost ten. I could pretend to be asleep.

But I'm not that guy.

[text: me] Yes. All good?

I see a dialogue bubble with three dots pop up. She's typing. Then it vanishes. She's stopped typing.

Finally, she starts again.

[text: Naomi] I'm still here
[text: Naomi] Hannsett I mean
[text: Naomi] can we talk?

I don't hesitate. I tell her to come over.

Twenty minutes later, there's a knock on my door. Naomi looks small standing in my doorway. Shoulders hunched, head tilted downward. Her sweater is knitted and has holes in the knitting.

She must be freezing.

"Hey," I say.

"Hey."

Her mascara is raccoon-dark around her eyes. She's been crying.

I let her in. She doesn't make herself at home. Instead, she takes a couple of steps inside and then stops, holding herself.

"Do you want a drink?" I ask.

"Please."

"Whiskey?"

"On the rocks."

I fix her a drink at my standing bar, but she hasn't moved from my foyer, jacket still wrapped around her shoulders.

I move to the couch. I pull a coaster forward on my table and set her drink on it, inviting her over. She takes the permission and sits on the couch beside me. Her bright orange sweater makes her stand out on the stark white couch.

Silence lingers between us. I'm okay with it.

I lift my glass, and she clinks hers against mine. We both take a sip.

She hasn't been here without Otto. Otto's room is like a separate entity, tucked away down the hall. He moved in after my mom passed away, and then it was like he just forgot to leave. I enjoy having him around, even if he exists like a squirrel. He stays in his room to write and occasionally only ventures out to grab something from the kitchen.

Since he started dating Naomi, he's been splitting time between both places. Naomi has spent the night a few times, but for the most part, he goes over to hers.

Now, it's strange to be here with her without Otto in it. I catch her staring at my house.

It's funny the things you take for granted. I've lived here three years. I'm used to it. But when Naomi's chin tilts, I see how it must look through her eyes.

Stained oak walls. A spacious, open-air floor plan. Long, slanted ceilings punctured with rectangular skylights.

It's a clean night. You can see stars through the skylight tonight, tiny dots pricking the black.

"Why do you have such a nice house?" Naomi asks.

The way she says it makes the edge of my mouth curl upward.

"What?" she says. "Did I say something funny?"

"No, it's just…" I smooth my hand down the leg of my trousers. "People don't really ask me that. They usually just… give me that look."

"What look?"

"That *what cartel are you associated with* look."

Elbow on her thigh, she perches her chin on the flat on her palm and curls her fingers around her lips. "Nah," she says. "You're too gentle for organized crime."

"I'll take that as a compliment." I clear my throat. "I was on a game show. *The Million Dollar Answer*."

Her eyes widen. "Did you win?"

I nod. "Yep."

"You must be like…next-level genius."

I chuckle softly. "Not really. The theme was pop culture and entertainment. Thirty questions. A million dollars. My mom…she worked part-time at the hotels. Turndown service. When I was a kid, I'd come with her, and she'd just sit me in front of the TV while she worked. So I became well versed in TV shows."

"Ho. Ly. Shit." She tilts her glass to her lips. The ice cubes clink around in her glass, but at least she's stopped shivering. She puts her glass down (she misses the coaster, but I'm not going to mention it). She finally takes her sweater off, letting it crumple behind her. "So you bought this house with the money?"

"With the remainder. First thing I did was pay off Mom's medical debt. That was like a guillotine over us."

"She must have been grateful."

"She was. And then she passed."

Naomi stares off into the distance. "Life is a bitch."

"Amen."

We both drink in the silence and the whiskey.

"My dad died when I was young," Naomi says. "He could've gotten treatment, but he refused it for religious reasons. This thing with Otto…it feels like that all over again. I can't watch another person I love leave this world with a chip on his shoulder." She sniffs then and presses the back of her hand to her nose. "I'm sorry—"

My heart breaks open for her. I reach over and set my hand on her leg.

"Naomi…"

She looks up at me. Unfallen tears shimmer in her eyes.

I wind my arm around her. She leans into my chest, curling herself into my body. I put my glass down (I also ignore the coaster—now is not the time for coasters). I take her in my arms and squeeze her tightly. She shakes with quiet sobs against my shoulder.

"I love you," Naomi says suddenly. She sniffles and wipes her nose on her sleeve. "I don't think people say that enough, you know? To the people they care about. When they're still…"

Still alive. That's what she means to say, but she can't get the words out.

"I know." I take her shoulders and squeeze them. "I love you, too."

20

JASON

I find Kenzi in the small waiting area on the third floor. It's an empty sea of chairs this late at night. She's sitting in the middle of a row, casually making her way through a Kit Kat bar.

Vending machine candy has always been her go-to stress snack.

She's staring off into space, dissociating. I don't blame her. It's been a long day for all of us.

I step over and sit beside her. "Hey. How's he doing?"

"The dialysis wiped him out. He's sleeping it off now, so I figured I'd wait out here."

"Sleep is good. He needs it. I brought the goods." I set the bags down at my feet. I touch each of them and recite, "Overnight clothes, daytime clothes, a couple of books, notebooks, pens, laptop, chargers...should be enough to keep him occupied for a while."

"You're a saint," Kenzi says as she looks through one of the bags. "Thank you. Seriously."

"Of course," I tell her. I do feel obligated to remind her, "Visiting hours are almost up."

"Well, tough shit. If Otto's spending the night here, so am I."

"Thought you'd say that." I pick up one of the bags and nudge it over to her. "Which is why *this* bag is yours."

"Smart man. You deserve a reward. Chocolate?" She offers me part of her chocolate bar.

I decline with a shake of my head. "Looks like you've got enough of it for the both of us."

I catch her bottom lip with my thumb and forefinger, wiping off a chocolate smear. I put my thumb to my mouth to lick it clean.

She grins at that.

It's a look that usually makes my blood start rushing south. Instead, I feel a small pinch of guilt in my gut. I rub my hand over the back of my neck. "I—uh. There's something we have to talk about. Not a big deal. It doesn't have to be now, but—"

Those green eyes size me up. "Jason. Just spit it out."

"Alright. Naomi tried to kiss me."

Kenzi blinks at me. Her mouth forms an O shape.

I feel a burning heat climb my neck and rise in my cheeks. "Obviously, I nipped it in the…well. I stopped it, is what I mean—"

And then Kenzi does something unexpected. She *laughs*.

Not like sweet giggles, either. She is *howling* with laughter.

"Is this funny to you?" I ask.

"Nu-uh! No! Very serious." She tries to pull a straight face. "I'm sorry. You were saying?"

"Okay…so she was in my car, and—"

Kenzi's bottom lip quivers. Her composure doesn't last for long. She clutches her stomach and explodes with another burst of laughter. There are tears streaming down her cheeks now.

The sharp slap of quickly approaching feet gets me to

look up from Kenzi. Donovan comes down the hall and stands in front of us. He looks at Kenzi, then at me, then Kenzi again.

"I thought someone was coding out here," he says. "What's so funny?"

"Honestly…I'm not sure," I say.

I genuinely don't know what to make of Kenzi's laughing fit.

Donovan has his arms folded. His finger taps impatiently against his bicep.

I try not to think about how, only hours ago, those long fingers were grabbing at me, digging into my back.

I fiddle with my wedding rings, twisting them around and around.

Kenzi wheezes. She wipes the laughter-tears away from her face and manages to get out, "Otto's girlfriend kissed Jason."

Donovan's expression hardens. There are daggers in his eyes when he says, "Where is she—?"

"No, no, no," Kenzi reasons with him, coming down from her laugh-attack. She winds her fingers in his hand and urges him closer. "We're not doing that. Come. Sit."

Donovan relents and sits. He takes the chair beside Kenzi.

Kenzi takes Donovan's hand in hers and then mine so she's the conduit between us.

"We're going to do an exercise," she says. "Meditation. Ready?"

"As I'll ever be," Donovan says.

"Good. Close your eyes. Inhale with me. Inhale the word: *What*."

The three of us take in a deep inhale. "*What*."

"Hold it," Kenzi continues. "And now exhale with these words: *The fuck*."

We inhale deeply. Hold. Exhale. "What…*the fuck?*"

"Feels better, doesn't it?"

I can't help but smile. "Yeah, actually."

For a minute, the three of us just sit there. Eyes closed. Holding hands.

"We're good parents," Kenzi murmurs suddenly. "Right?"

I open my eyes. Kenzi's eyes are still closed, her head tilted back. Donovan's are open, however. He looks at me when he says, "We're the best."

Then he squeezes her hand a little tighter. I can feel it, as though his palm is against mine.

I lace my fingers between Kenzi's. She smiles.

This feels right. The three of us.

The way it should be.

21

OTTO

There's a face staring up at me.

Banana slices for eyes. A wide, blueberry smile. Pancake dough cheeks.

The master touch: two bacon eyebrows.

"Be careful, the plate is hot," mom warns me as she places utensils in front of me.

The plate is hot because my breakfast gets reheated in the oven. I'm fifteen, permanently exhausted, and can't pull myself out of bed before noon. Well after everyone else has been served.

"Thanks," I mumble. I'm only half awake as I slice into my breakfast-slash-lunch.

I eat on the kitchen island as mom does the dishes. Outside, the Hannsett Island summer sun is blaring through the windows. We have a small backyard that you can cross to get to the beach. Jason and Donovan are outside playing with Joan. Some 90s band is blaring on the outdoor speaker as a frisbee zips back and forth between the two men. Joan wobbles on pudgy legs, following the frisbee one way, then the other, her little hands reaching for it.

Jason sounds a victorious war cry when Donovan misses the catch. I wince at the sound.

"Do they have to be so loud in the morning?"

"It stopped being morning two hours ago, buddy."

I scowl and shove a syrupy bite in my mouth. "It's still annoying."

"Be nice to Daddy Jason. He's a little bummed today."

"Why?"

"He lost one of his patients last night."

Lost. Like someone is going to retrieve the dead person in the hospital's lost-and-found bin.

He doesn't look like he lost anything. He's soaking in the summer sun, tossing a frisbee back and forth.

But Jason has always been good at hiding sadness behind a smile. I guess we have that in common.

"What happens when we die?" I blurt out suddenly.

I watch my mom's back. I can't see her expression because she's facing the window, but her shoulders stiffen.

"I don't know," she answers honestly. When she turns back to face me, she has a smile on now. There it is again. Sadness, meet smile. "*But,*" she adds, "I hope where ever we go, we get to eat all the bacon we want."

I look down at my breakfast plate. It's suddenly piled high with bacon.

Fear tickles up my spine like a cold hand.

This isn't right.

This food is not real. The sun is not shining. I'm not fifteen.

"Mom?"

"Yes, baby?"

"Am I...dead?"

Mom dries her hands to come beside me, leaning against the counter. She takes a piece of bacon and crunches it.

"Not yet." She says conversationally, her tone light.

Not yet. Her words echo in the silence.

Silence.

Joan has stopped cackling. I look out the window, but they're gone.

So is summer.

It's snowing. Nothing but thick, white snow covering the windows. Wiping out the world like a giant eraser.

"Where is everyone?"

"We're all waiting for you." My mom touches my face. Her thumb rubs softly over my cheek. "Waiting for you to wake the hell up."

* * *

I jerk awake.

The morning light cuts across Naomi's bedroom.

Milo has made a nest out of the sweaters piled on her round chair and is curled up in a puddle of sunlight.

It's cold with the heat still busted, but we're warm. My body is slotted against Diego's, his arm around my middle. He's as cozy as a fireplace. Naomi is tucked against my chest. Their legs are tangled up with mine, and I can't tell where one person stops and the next begins.

When I shift, Naomi blinks her eyes open. Those soft brown eyes light up when I meet her gaze.

She rubs her hand over my chest.

"It's okay," she yawns. "It's just a nightmare."

Her armor is off. We're both bare like this, hearts spilled open first thing in the morning, our love like a broken yoke.

Her smile is gentle, and sleepy, and all mine.

"You okay?" she asks.

I nod. "I am now."

"I love you, Otto."

"I love you—"

* * *

"—*Naomi.*"

I reach for her, but she's not there. Neither is Diego.

I wake myself up with her name on my lips.

My bed is empty. My sheets are stiff. This room is too clean and smells faintly like bleach and medicine. Beside me, a machine bleeps rhythmically, marking my heart rate.

I'm in the hospital. And I'm alone.

But I'm awake. Really awake this time.

I think.

This is what you wanted. Lock up the pity party.

I close my eyes again and exhale a deep breath.

I've typed out maybe twenty texts to Naomi.

I'm sorry. I miss you. Please come back.

But every time I type out the words, I delete them before I can send them.

My chest aches. I try to ignore the heaviness in my heart and take stock of the rest of my body instead. My Poisonous Friend throbs uncomfortably at my side. If I stay very, very still, I can almost ignore the pain.

Is this what the rest of my life will be? Holding my body like a mug of hot coffee on a pitching boat. Doing everything in my power to keep the discomfort from spilling everywhere.

A sharp lash of pain comes on. I push my fingers into the mattress and exhale a shuddery breath.

Breathe through it. It'll be over soon.

It's finally subsiding when my phone vibrates beside me. I blink bruised spots from my eyes and swipe my phone from its spot on my bed.

My first thought is: *Naomi? Diego?*

No. Neither.

It's my sister. I open the text. It says:

[text: Joan] Mr. Bones says hello.

Despite the pain, a small grin finds its way over my mouth.

She's here.

It's nearly midnight, but she's here.

I glance around. I'm not about to bother the nurses. I remove the monitor from my finger, ignoring the way it makes the machine go nuts. There are suitcases filled with my clothes at the foot of the bed. I rid myself of the hospital gown and slip into a black shirt and gray sweatpants instead. The waistband doesn't put too much pressure on my abdomen, and with "real people clothes" on now, I feel slightly more normal.

I put on my shoes, tuck my phone in my back pocket, and quietly slip out of my hospital room. There's a nurses' desk around the corner to my right. Even this late at night, there's a light murmur of activity there. I don't want to be ushered back into my room, so I hang a left instead, toward the stairs.

I pass by a small sectioned-off waiting room. My feet momentarily come to a halt here.

Ah. There they are.

My mom, Jason, and Donovan have all fallen asleep together in the waiting room. My mom is slumped to her side, her head on Donovan's shoulder. Donovan is nestled against her. Jason has his arm around my mom's shoulders, his head tilted back.

This is how I'm used to seeing them. Not this bullshit keep-your-distance dance they've been doing with each other over the past couple of months.

I'm used to seeing them piled up like puppies, wrapped in each other.

The sight of it makes my heart pinch.

They look too peaceful, so I don't wake them. I just walk past them quietly and make my way to the stairwell.

We're only on the third floor, but it takes me longer than normal to hobble down to the first.

I spent a lot of my young life at this hospital. But Joan *grew up* here. With both our dads working here, she'd often come to work and spend the day in daycare or be passed between the two of them whenever one finished a shift.

There is a part of me that's always envied her for that. I made a family. I experienced the growing pains of their triad. Donovan and Jason had to learn to be fathers with me.

By the time Joan entered the picture, it was all smooth sailing. She's only ever known a life with one mom, two dads, and me. She's never had to question her place in it.

I might've resented her for it, if she wasn't so dang cute.

The day she was born, my heart melted in my chest. I knew I was going to spend the rest of my life loving and protecting this tiny creature with everything I had in me.

Over the years, the both of us developed an intimate knowledge of the ins and outs of the hospital. It was, after all, her playground. I spent a lot of time playing hide-and-seek with her in these halls—and getting into a fair amount of trouble when I lost her in the ICU.

I get down to the first floor, move past the elevators, and down the hall. I push open a closed door and find it unlocked. It opens up to a mini rec room, complete with a table, fridge, a sink, and a row of lockers. There's an empty conference room adjoining.

This space is mostly for hosting students for training sessions and workshops. *Doctors of Tomorrow* is one of the hospital's more well-known study programs for promising upcoming medical students to get their hands dirty. The program has been running for decades.

This room is, also, one of Joan's favorite places to hide.

Mr. Bones is a display skeleton propped up in the corner of the room. A teaching tool. He has his hand lifted toward the door, his middle finger pointing up while the rest are folded down.

Yep. Joan has definitely been here.

"Okay, wild one," I say. "Where are you hiding?"

I check under the table. Behind the door.

Nada.

I scan the lockers. I start opening them up, one by one.

"I swear, if you're in here—"

"Arrrgh!" Joan shouts as she leaps out from a locker just as I open it, her arms raised.

I hear myself shout. "Bloody Jesus *fuck*!"

Even if I was anticipating it, my heart still leaps into my throat.

Her dark hair looks wild around her head. She frowns, her lower lip ring protruding.

"That's a hell of a way to greet your little sister."

I open my arms. "Alright. Come."

She flings herself at me. Too hard. For someone only an inch or two over five feet, she's a cannonball. I wince at her hug.

"Ouch."

Quickly, she retracts. "Yikes. Sorry. Where does it hurt?"

"Everywhere."

"Baby."

"Brat."

She grins at that.

My parents named Joan after Joan Jett. Joan took the namesake and ran with it. She's a punk rock princess. Thick black hair that she keeps in a messy chop around her shoulders. Torn jeans and a leather jacket laden with pins that read her like bumper stickers. She has her bottom lip pierced, as well as piercings up and down her ears and probably in places I don't want to know about.

Ever since she turned eighteen earlier this year, she's been threatening to get a tattoo. The only problem is she can't commit to any concept longer than a couple of days before she scraps it and goes back to the drawing board.

She has Mom's eyes. Emerald green, like sea glass.

Privately, though I'd never admit it out loud, I think I was always grateful that she looks more like Mom than Donovan.

"This is new." A tap my finger against a new piercing—an eyebrow stud above her left eye.

She tilts back on her heels, leaning away from my prodding. "Believe it or not, things change."

"Oh yeah? You're a sophisticated woman in London?"

"Fuck yeah. New school. New friends. New me."

"New partner?" I loop my finger around her necklace. It's a simple silver chain, but it has a ring hanging from it. "What is this, a promise ring?"

Her eyes flash. "How about you mind your own business?"

Spitfire. All five feet of her.

And she'd probably rather spend the holidays with her new beloved instead of stuck in a hospital.

My mouth pinches into a frown. "I'm sorry you had to come back here."

"What, you think I'd miss this? I'm sort of the star actress. Would be pretty shitty to be a no-show to my own transplant."

All levity leaves my voice. I need her to know I'm serious when I tell her, "You know you don't have to do this."

"If my options are *lose a brother* or *lose a kidney*, I pick *lose a kidney*. I've got two of those and only one dumbass brother."

"Gee, thanks." I snort a laugh.

"Besides. I've been keeping this baby nice and juicy for you. I can go to bars in London, you know. Drinking age is eighteen. Do you know how many free drinks I turn down on a regular basis?"

"There's something wrong with you."

"Duh." She reaches down and links her pinky in mine. "I've been prepping for this my entire life. I'm in. I think the real question is…are *you* ready?"

It hits me all at once. I know I have to give up the kidney if I want any sort of future with Naomi and Diego.

But, oh, god. It's hard.

It hits me all at once. All the emotion I've been bottling up inside.

I clutch my side, double over, and cry. My sister wraps her arms around me, holding on to me.

"It's okay," she murmurs. "It's all going to be okay."

PART III

CHRISTMAS DAY. DECEMBER 25TH

22

DIEGO

Christmas morning is always cold.
Fresh snow is falling outside. It's piled up on the windowsill, blocking out the sunlight.

Naomi is soft in my arms.

She spent the night in one of my shirts. It swallows her. Still, it looks good on her.

I press a kiss to the top of her head, but she doesn't move. Gently, I unwind my arms from her and peel out.

I've got a pair of PJ pants on. I have slippers under my bed, and I put those on as well.

We were good last night. PG.

We kissed, but that was all. Anything more wouldn't have felt right. Not when we were both heavy with emotion, like sponges that have yet to be squeezed out.

Holding her felt good, though. Soul-healing. We both needed it, I think. More than we knew, maybe.

She's deep asleep. Her lips are parted, her eyebrows relaxed. I pet her hair back from her face and then get to my feet. Quietly, I exit the bedroom, leaving the door just slightly ajar. I go into my kitchen instead. I've got an automatic coffee machine, so I pop a pod in and open my cabinet.

I pick out my favorite mug—the race car. I make myself a cup of coffee, a little sugar, a little cream. Then I carry it with me to the window and watch the snow fall.

My windows are long, floor-to-ceiling fixtures. In the summer, I get to watch sailboats cruise across the ocean. Now, my view is wiped clean. As though someone took a big eraser and got rid of all of Hannsett Island.

Nothing but me and Naomi left.

"God, that's beautiful," she says.

I glance over my shoulder. Naomi has crawled out of the bedroom. She curls up on my couch, pulling a quilt over her bare legs to keep warm. Like me, she's watching the snowfall. I don't care who you are—it's impossible not to get entranced by the falling snow.

"Yeah," I tell her. "It is."

She smiles at me. Then she nods toward my coffee. "Think you can make one of those for me?"

I almost go to the kitchen, and then I hesitate. I stare at the mug in my hand.

I make a choice.

"You can have this one," I tell her. I hold it out for her to take.

"Thanks." She wraps her hands around the race car and tilts the mug to her lips.

She'll keep it safe. I can trust her with things that are important to me. I can let go. And it does feel good, seeing it in her hands.

Just then, my phone buzzes.

I pull it out of my pocket and check my texts. I feel a smile slowly draw over my lips.

"Good news?" Naomi asks. I can hear the hopeful note in her voice.

"It's a Christmas miracle." I lift my eyes to meet hers. "Otto is getting a new kidney."

PART IV

THE TATTOO. DECEMBER 28TH

23

NAOMI

*I*t's late, but New York City is still bustling outside. I close my eyes, lean back in my tattoo station, and pinch the bridge of my nose to ward off a pending migraine.

It's been one of those days.

Christmas Day, Otto got a kidney transplant. The surgery lasted all day, and that night, Diego reported, he and his sister came out of the operating room safe and sound.

Which is great for them. But it was time for me to put my feet back on solid ground.

I took the LIRR back to New York City. I took a shower. I fed Milo. I went back to work.

It's been four days and I haven't heard a peep from Otto.

We're short-staffed at both the coffee shop and the tattoo parlor for the holidays. Which is fine by me. I need to keep busy.

The second I stop for a breather, my heart feels like it's going to split in two.

Heartache has apparently morphed into *headache*. I'm the last man standing at the tattoo shop, and I allow myself a second before I start to clean up.

The front doorbell chimes, alerting me that someone's walked in.

I push up to my feet, exiting my stall. "Hey, we're closing. You'll have to come back…"

But my *later* dies in my throat.

Because it's not just any customer.

Otto stands in the front of the shop. The pink neon sign from the window blares behind him. His dark slacks hang from his slim hips. A white shirt comes down loosely around his tall frame. He smiles, but it's crooked.

"Sorry," he says. "The sign said Closed, but I was hoping you'd make an exception."

He's alive. On his feet. I want nothing more than to run to him and wrap my arms around him.

But I hold myself back. I hug myself instead.

"Shouldn't you still be at the hospital?" I ask him.

He shrugs. "They let me out on good behavior."

"Ha."

The silence lingers between us. On the radio, they're still playing Christmas songs.

Those bastards.

"I heard the surgery went well," I say, filling in the spots.

He nods. "I'm in one piece."

He limps a little when he walks, though. He's not completely healed.

He shouldn't be here. His body hurts. My heart hurts. We're just going to keep hurting each other.

I try a smile. "Well. Good. You really didn't have to come all the way here."

"Actually. I did." Those blue eyes go serious, suddenly. It's a new look for him. "I keep thinking about our last conversation, and—"

I hold up a hand to stop him. "You don't have to apologize. You told me from day one…you're not the kind of guy who makes commitments. I'm the one who let her feelings get away from her. So. I think it's best we just…go our separate ways."

His eyes are bright in the dark of the empty studio. "The problem is…I can't let you go."

I knit my eyebrows. "Otto…"

"I was an asshole to you. I lied to you. I pushed you away. You loved me hard, and I got scared."

I press my lips together. "So what's changed? Because I can't stop loving you. And you can't commit. It just sounds like we're at an impasse."

"Well. Maybe not."

I swallow. My emotions are doing a tightrope act, and I have to dig my nails into my arms to keep my vision from blurring. "Don't say that unless you mean it."

"I want to commit. To you."

He sounds so earnest when he says it. So genuine. But…

"How am I supposed to believe that?"

"Let me prove it to you."

With that, he closes the distance between us. Then he helps himself into my station and sits up on my big client's chair.

"Give me a tattoo," he says. "Anywhere. Whatever you want. If you want to write *Asshole* across my forehead, do it. I deserve it. Whatever it is, I want to think about you every time I look at it." He takes my hand in his. He squeezes. "I want you to be with me for the rest of my life. Whatever that looks like."

I stare at him. Then an idea hits me.

I step away from him. I get out my tattoo gun, load it up, and then hold out my hand.

"Give me your hand." He does, resting his hand on mine. I look up at him. "This is going to hurt like a bitch."

Otto swallows. "I'm ready."

The machine buzzes as I flick it on.

PART V

NEW YEARS' EVE. DECEMBER 31ST

24

DIEGO

Christmas bells are ringing...

Okay, not exactly Christmas bells.

We're calling it "Newmas." A New Year's/Christmas blend to make up for the time missed out.

Otto spent Christmas day in surgery. Now he's laid out on our living room couch, cups of water, Advil, and pill bottles littering the coffee table.

To Otto's credit, he's in good spirits. He's in pj's and a Santa hat, which is too big on his head and droops to one side.

Naomi spent the night—as she's done every night since the two of them came back from the city, Otto with a bandage wrapped around his hand. He's healed since, and now he wears the tattoo of a monkey with a Christmas hat on the back of his hand—a permanent reminder of our night at the holiday concert. This morning, the three of us got up, had coffee and muffins, and opened up presents from under the tree. Now, I've got wrapping paper scattered over the floor, coffee rings on my table, and one Otto who can barely keep his eyes open.

I'm on one side of the couch, Otto's feet in my lap, and

Naomi sits on the opposite end, his head on her legs. She rests her arm around him and pets her fingers absently over the scruffy beard that's begun to sprout up over his jaw.

"What do you think?" Naomi asks. "Successful Newmas?"

"*Great* Newmas," Otto murmurs. "We should do this every year."

He's not lying. We are spoiled—our opened presents sit under the tree. A blank notebook for Otto to write in. A new sweater for me. A pair of earrings for Naomi, and a cat toy for Milo.

Otto's eyelids get heavy. He stares at the lights of the Christmas tree, trying to keep his eyes open. Failing.

I give his toes a small squeeze.

"Hey. How are you feeling?"

Those blue eyes open again. "Tired. And in pain." He yawns and stretches out, his toes briefly digging into my thighs. "And horny."

I can't help but chuckle. "You got major surgery…and your first to-do item is to fuck?"

"Always. I'm pent-up. But like…moving hurts."

"How about jerking off? Can you do that?"

"I think so…"

Otto reaches underneath the band of his sweatpants. I can see the outline of his hand, lazily moving up and down.

He sighs. "Yep. That works."

Naomi bites her bottom lip. Her eyes twinkle like Christmas lights. "Fuck," she murmurs. "Do you know how much that turns me on?"

Otto tilts his head back against her thigh, looking up at her face. "Show me."

Her eyes locked on his, she unbuttons her zipper and then reaches underneath her pants. Her eyes flutter once as she fondles herself. She sighs deeply, contently, and then retracts her hand.

Her fingers are glistening. The sight makes my throat tight with want.

And I'm not the only one. Otto takes her wrist in his hand and guides her fingers into his mouth. He sucks one digit, then the next. "You taste so good," he murmurs. He's hoarse with want. "I need more."

He tugs on her pants. Naomi shifts in her spot, lifting her hips to roll her pants off her legs. She climbs on top of Otto then, straddling his face. Her eyes meet mine, and she takes the back of my head, pulling me into a kiss.

I love her lips. I love her softness. I love the way she gasps into my mouth, and I know Otto's tongue is inside of her, consuming her.

This is the lazy, Christmas morning sex that the three of us deserve.

I draw my lips down Naomi's jaw and neck. She whimpers into my kisses as she rocks her hips over Otto's face. He's gripping her thighs, drawing her nearer, and I can hear his muffled moan between her legs.

I dip my head down. Otto's shirt rides up, revealing that fresh scar across his abdomen. The skin around it is red and sensitive, and I avoid that area completely. Instead, I gently pull his sweatpants down, just enough to let his cock spring free.

He wasn't lying about being pent-up. He's already so erect, so swollen.

Tenderly, I kiss the tip of him. I draw a line of kisses downward, to the base.

I haven't done this before. But I want to.

I lick him. Tasting. The skin here is velvet smooth. When I get to the tip of him, I taste the ocean.

Otto groans. He pushes his hips forward, toward my mouth. But I take his thighs in my hands, firmly pinning him down.

"Don't move," I tell him, the doctor in me taking over. "Or you're going to pop a stitch."

"*Uck*." Otto's swear is muffled, especially when Naomi folds her knees completely so she's sitting on his chin.

Her dark bush matches the color of his beard. They look like one being.

With Otto's legs pinned between me, I take his cock into my mouth. I remember how he sucked me—the low, swooping momentum—and I try to mimic it. But when I try to suck him down, he touches the back of my throat, and I gag. Instead, I take his base in my hand and swallow as much of him as I comfortably can, breathing through my nose.

This seems to be a good thing, because the muscles of his abdomen go tight, and he trembles underneath me.

I let myself explore Otto with my tongue and my lips. I suck. I lick. I savor the sweet-salt taste of him.

"Oh god, oh god, oh my *god*."

I open my eyes and turn them upward. Naomi is climaxing in front of me. Her thighs shake, lower lip buttoned between her teeth.

She's watching me as she unravels. It's intoxicatingly erotic to watch her eyes get wide and her cheeks go red with a blush, as though she's been caught with her hand in the cookie jar.

It makes me throb.

She moans, and the sound is almost pained as her hips give another shuddery thrust.

Naomi's hair is pulled back. Her hair tie has jingle bells on it, and every time she moves against Otto's mouth, the little bells chime.

It gives me an idea.

I lift my head, dropping Otto from my mouth. That gets a deep groan from him.

"Jesus…fucking Christ, Diego," Otto whines as Naomi

lifts off him. His Santa hat has fallen from his head, and his lips are glistening and swollen and pink.

His cock pulses in my hand at the absence of my mouth. I didn't realize how close I'd gotten him.

Uh...whoops.

I feel a tinge of guilt but mostly pride. *I did that*.

I clear my throat and look at Naomi. "Do you think you can cum again?"

She blinks at me. Her eyes are still half-lidded, but her lips draw into a smile. "Only one way to find out."

I open my palm out to her. "Can I have your hair tie?"

Her eyebrows quirk upward. But she slides it off her hair, letting the thick strands fall down her back. Then she drops it into my hand.

"Do you want to fuck Naomi?" I ask Otto.

He flashes me a look. "Yeah, but I have an overbearing nurse who keeps complaining about my stitches."

I chuckle. I take her jingle bell hair tie and fit it around Otto's wrist. It jingles when he moves.

"Here," I tell him. "You set the pace. Show me how you want me to fuck her."

Otto's eyes light up at that. He grins. "Let the virgin out the bottle and he becomes a kink-fucking-genie."

I rise from my spot to stand in front of Naomi. I take her face in my hand and stroke my thumb over her cheek. "Is that good for you?"

"Yeah." She smirks. "Very good."

She pushes her mouth against mine. I feel her fingers tug the drawstring of my pants. She massages me over them, and the friction draws a sigh from me.

I cradle her body, scoop her up in my arms, and lift her to gently set her down on the carpeted floor. I slot my body on top of hers, kissing her, and fit myself between her thighs.

Here, Otto has a perfect view of us. Already, I can hear the light jangle of the bells as Otto takes himself in his hand.

It's intimate. The way Naomi pulls my shirt off and rubs her hands up my chest. The way her lips butterfly against my throat. The way she sighs when I ease myself inside of her, already slick from Otto's tongue.

And it's erotic. It sends a heat through my blood when I look up and see Otto watching us, those blue eyes hazy with desire.

He strokes himself slowly. From base to tip and back again.

Jingle...jingle...jingle...

I move to his beat. I make love to Naomi as she spreads out onto the white carpet with the softest moan. I clutch her thigh, holding her open. Her Christmas sweater hikes up her chest, revealing the soft underside of her breasts.

All three of us have been tested and cleared. And it's worth it to feel the wet, naked heat of Naomi's body as she clings to me.

"Oh, god," Naomi murmurs. "That feels so good."

Otto picks up the pace.

Jingle-jingle...jingle-jingle...

I groan. Naomi's fingers tighten on my shoulders, her nails digging into me.

She's already orgasmed once, but I can feel it building inside of her again, her body growing tight.

"Fuck," she swears. She reaches between us, and the back of her hand tickles my abdomen as she flicks her clit rapidly.

My breath is light, and I close my eyes, concentrating, forcing myself to hold back. I bite the inside of my lip.

Jinglejinglejingle!

The beat is too fast for me to pull back now. I'm pounding her to keep pace. I moan loudly as I explode inside of Naomi.

She cries out. Her thighs tremble, and her hips thrust upward a couple of times before I feel her pulse around me, pulling me, drawing my own orgasm out.

Naomi mewls and grabs my face. She kisses me frantically, and I feel myself returning it, sloppily plunging my tongue in her mouth.

Otto swears from his spot on the couch. He stops jingling, and when I open my eyes, I can see him holding his softening cock, lips parted, panting, white glistening across his belly.

"Good god," Otto pants. "Ho-ho-*ho* indeed."

Naomi laughs. She grabs a throw pillow and tosses it at his face. "Dumbass."

He smirks at her. "Slut."

There's love in his eyes, though.

So much love. Love in his gaze. Love in Naomi's touch. Love in my chest, spilling out over both of them.

Love, love, *love*.

"I love you," I blurt out. My gaze goes to Naomi, then Otto, then back. "Both of you."

Naomi smiles. She gently runs her fingers through my hair and down the back of my neck. "I love you, too."

"I love you three," Otto replies. I lift my eyebrows at him. He always has to get a joke in.

But when my eyes meet his, I know he means it.

There's a boyish grin on his lips but serious intention in his gaze. He holds my gaze, and I need him suddenly. I shift my body to bridge the small gap between us and brush my lips against his. He takes me in a kiss that doesn't hesitate or waver. This time, he doesn't pull away from me. There's confidence in his kiss. Devotion.

He tastes like Naomi, and Otto, and *us*. I savor it.

"Merry Newmas," Otto murmurs as we break apart.

I smile. "Merry Newmas."

25

KENZI

The Anchor is popping with their annual New Year's festivities.

Karaoke plays out on the stage. Locals sing along and laugh. Everyone is wearing some kind of decorative glasses or hats and holding on to noisemakers.

Meanwhile, I'm hanging on to the bar as though it's the last lifesaver on the *Titanic*. I've only had one glass of wine, and I sip it slowly, but it's hitting me like I've had ten.

It's been a long year, and it's finally catching up with me.

I should be over the moon. Otto finally agreed to the surgery. It went off without a hitch. Both he and Joan are recovering smoothly. As a silver-lining bonus, I got my little girl back home for the holidays. Sure, she's spending it healing from her childhood bedroom, but. I'll take silver linings where I can get them.

Everything turned out like it should. And *yet*…

I'm exhausted.

Jason breaks through the crowd and comes to stand beside me. He's just finished a rousing rendition of *NSYNC's "I Want You Back."

Nothing—and I mean *nothing*—can come between Jason and karaoke night.

He gets behind me and winds his arms around my middle. "Are you having fun?"

I smile and shrug. "Eh."

I'm not about to lie to him. And I don't have to.

He hunches over to rest his chin on my shoulder. "Do you want to go home, wrap up in blankets, and watch the ball drop on TV instead?"

I gasp, swivel around, and rest my hand on Jason's chest. "Is this…dirty talk? Because it's kind of turning me on."

Jason snorts on a laugh. "Happy New Year, Trouble."

"Happy New Year, Hotshot."

Jason presses a kiss to my lips, then a second.

We're always kissing in doubles these days. Making up for our lost third.

I twist back around so I'm facing the bar. When the bartender looks my way, I wave him down with my wallet. "Can I please close out?"

He shakes his head. "You're covered."

I lift an eyebrow at Jason, but he shrugs. "Don't look at me."

The bartender slides a piece of paper across the bar. "Guy who paid left this for you."

I flip the note over.

It says, in tight, familiar handwriting, *Meet me at the Lighthouse*.

I bite my lip and glance at Jason. "Up for an adventure?"

I hold up the note for him to read. I watch a smile cross his face when it clicks.

"Let's go," he says.

I wind my fingers in his and tug Jason out of the bar.

It's cold outside. Bitterly. The frigid wind curls up from the glass-like ocean and whips off the clifftop, burrowing through my wool layers.

Jason must notice me shivering because seconds later, his jacket hangs over my shoulders, swallowing me.

I squint at him. He's wearing only his long-sleeved button-up now. He shrugs. "I run hot."

Liar.

I'm too cold not to take the jacket, though.

The parking lot is lit, but I walk us behind the bar. It's a short climb to the lighthouse up ahead, but the foot of snow on the ground means it takes twice as long to get there.

The Hannsett Island Lighthouse is old. A tall, red structure that is, for the most part, out of commission. They light it up for the holidays, though. There's a string of wreaths around the lighthouse, giving it a little holiday spirit.

Normally, it's locked up. But when I yank the old door, it pops open.

It's quiet in here. The sound of the door closing echoes up the steep, hollow inside. There are a couple of candlelit lanterns in the entranceway, but most of the dim light emanates from the string lights that crawl up the twisted, spiral staircase.

It's breath-catchingly romantic in here.

"Hasn't changed much, has it?" Jason says as he tilts his head to look around.

The last time we were here, Jason, Donovan, and I were just getting to know each other. Well. *Re-know* each other. Jason, in one of his grand, romantic gestures, had booked the inn at the lighthouse for all three of us. We'd spent the night clinging to each other.

Now, the tables have turned.

"Come on," I tell Jason. I tug his hand and climb the stairs.

We do loops upward until we're almost at the top. There's a blue door here, and when I try it, it opens up and lets us in.

The room is exactly as I remember it. Cottage baby blues with white trim. Seashells and nautical-themed decorations.

Giant circular windows overlooking the midnight sea and star-spackled sky. A wide, king-sized bed.

And there he is. Donovan sits on the edge of the bed. He's New Year's ready, in a crimson blazer and crisp black button-up. His ruddy brown hair is brushed forward in a stylish swoop. His trimmed beard outlines his jaw. And then there are those items he never, ever removes—his twin leather bracelets and his own double wedding band snug around his ring finger.

Donovan rarely dresses up. But he's cleaned up. For us. For this.

That act alone makes my heart flip in my chest.

He's wringing his hands together, but he stops when he sees us. Those dark brown eyes look up, achingly hopeful. Relieved to see us. And he pulls a small, nervous smile.

"Hey."

"Dude!" Jason says, crashing through the delicate moment like a bull in a china shop. "This is romantic as shit!"

Donovan winces. "Is it too much?"

"No." I grin. I step over in front of Donovan and put my hands on his thighs. I lean in and press a small, simple kiss to his mouth. "It's perfect."

His shoulders relax a little, but I can tell he's still on edge. He laces his fingers together again, tenting his hands, then folding them. "Can we...talk for a second?"

Jason, as distractible as a golden retriever, is already stuck on the window, looking out at the beautiful view below.

"Check it out. You can see the Big Dipper."

I slip my hand into Jason's. I steer him back, and the two of us sit on a bench across from Donovan.

"Yes," I say, turning all my attention to Donovan. "We're listening."

Donovan clears his throat. I'm certain he's practiced this moment. But now he's nervous, like a kid standing on the stage for their first opening night show.

"Okay," he starts. "Well. First...thanks for showing up. Both of you. I know I've been a pain in the ass—"

"You've been sad," I tell him. "You don't have to apologize for being sad."

"I'm not," he says firmly. "This isn't an apology." His gaze averts. "Not exactly, anyway. This is me saying...thank you. Thank you for giving me space. Thank you for understanding. Thank you for being the best partners I could ask for. Better than I deserve.

"Yes. I've been sad. I spent a lot of this year in pain. And instead of letting you two in...I pushed you away. Both of you." Donovan's gaze turns to Jason. "Especially you, Jason."

Jason shakes his head. "You were just doing what you had to—"

"Wait. Let me finish." Donovan exhales a deep breath. "Let me just...get this out before I lose my nerve, and then you can say whatever you need. I need you to know that I never stopped loving the two of you. I never stopped believing in us. The three of us. But I did stop loving myself. That changed my relationship with you. And with Otto. I sent our whole family through a loop. It hurt all of us, whether I intended it or not. And for that...I'm sorry."

He glances down. He sniffs, though I can tell he's trying to hold it together.

"I don't expect to come home right away. I know this past month has been on my timeline. But...I'm ready now. I'd love to come back home. On your timeline. I know these things take time, I just...um..."

His voice cracks, and he swallows hard. He's clearly fighting back the urge to cry.

"I'm ready to be an *us* again," he finally gets out. His voice is small. Quiet.

Enough. I sit down next to him and put my hand on his thigh.

"Donovan...the only person keeping you away is *you*. You

could come back anytime. The house is yours. Ours. We want you there."

Donovan glances at Jason, searching for confirmation. Jason comes and sits down on the other side of Donovan, mirroring me.

"It's true," Jason says. "Come home." Then he knocks his leg against the other man's. "Asshole."

Donovan snorts a laugh. As usual, Jason's inability to stay serious for more than a couple of minutes at a time gives us all the permission to breathe. Before we know it, all three of us are laughing.

"Fuck," Donovan says and presses the heel of his palm into his eye. "I missed you."

"I missed you, too." I lean forward and Donovan meets me halfway. Our lips touch.

It sends a shiver through me.

When Jason kisses me, I feel loved. Protected. Cared for.

When Donovan kisses me, I feel known.

We're soul mates—always have been, ever since we were teenagers—and when he deepens the kiss, I feel a very large missing piece of my heart settle back into place.

"I need you," I whisper against his mouth. His breath shudders against my cheek. Jason kisses the back of his neck, and their fingers entwine on Donovan's thigh.

For the longest time, the three of us just exchange a language of kisses, inhaling each other. Double hands make easy work of our clothes, and before long, we're naked, bare skin kissing bare skin kissing bare skin.

The sheets are silky against my back. Donovan's lips map out my body. They touch my hip, the soft swell of my stomach, that low scar where Joan was extracted from me. His lips travel upward as he climbs over me, and I sigh as I move my hands over his ass, pulling him snugly against me. His hard length nestles against my abdomen, and I push my hips upward, wanting.

Jason hovers over Donovan and kisses the other man's shoulder, the back of his neck. "Where's the—?"

"Left of the bed."

Jason reaches over the bed and pulls up a bottle of lube. "Copy that."

Jason snuggles up in bed beside me. He's made of muscles, and I find myself kissing his bicep, nibbling his arm.

Jason squirts a dollop of lube onto his fingers and then reaches between me and Donovan. I feel his hand curl at my pelvis. His large fingers rub against my slit, coating me.

Donovan kisses my throat, Jason nuzzles against my ear. I'm covered in my husbands, and I love it.

"Is that what you want, baby?" Jason purrs in my ear.

"Yeah..."

He dips a finger inside of me, and I gasp at the welcome intrusion. Those surgeon's hands know me far too well, and the slight crook of his finger has my toes curling into the sheets.

I only get it for a moment, though. He retracts his hand, and I whimper. Donovan's breath is hot on my shoulder, and I hear him groan as Jason takes his cock in his hand, spreading the lube between us. Jason and Donovan kiss, their mouths meeting sloppily, hungrily, and the sight of it makes me throb.

Once we're both slick and buzzing with pleasure, Jason pushes off the mattress. He climbs on top of Donovan now, their bodies fitting together.

Donovan's mouth covers mine. I stroke my fingers through his hair as he eases himself inside of me. He's a perfect fit—he feels swollen and thick inside of me but not uncomfortably so. Like our bodies were meant to merge together. I wind my legs around his hips and wrap my arms around his shoulders. I grip skin; my nails find Jason's back, the two of them folded together.

"I love you," I whisper, the words falling from me as Donovan's thrust sends a wave of pleasure through me.

"I love you, too," Donovan murmurs against my mouth, his words as sweet as honey.

"I love you," Jason says to both of us and repeats for good measure, "I love you, I love you…"

Jason's strong hand clutches the headboard, and he and Donovan move together as one—Jason inside of Donovan, Donovan inside of me. We're together, the three of us, and I feel so connected to them like this. It sends a hot rush of pleasure through me that makes me dizzy with it.

Donovan moans, his eyebrows crushed together, and his skin is so hot, a light sheen of sweat making us slide together. He takes my hands suddenly and pins them to the pillow by my head. Jason's hands cover Donovan's, both their fingers curling, and now I'm completely pinned underneath both of them. I gasp, suffocating on my own ecstasy, as my body becomes taut as a violin string—singing, humming, vibrating. Donovan swings his hips slow and low, his pelvis rolling against mine in a way that rubs against my swollen nub, and I grind against the edge of my pleasure.

I whimper with each breath. My husbands move against me in waves. I want this to last—oh, god, I want this to last forever. But my heels are digging into the mattress, and my fingers tighten between theirs.

"Oh, god," I whimper.

"Let go, Kenzi," Donovan murmurs in a low, rough growl.

My body obeys. I throw my head back and shout as my orgasm erupts through me, pulsing, pulling. I'm the ocean. I'm the night sky. I'm endless, and the two loves of my life are pouring into me, filling me.

We sweat and pant and slide together, a mess of limbs and sloppy kisses. *I love these men.* It's a love so strong that it makes my whole body warm and lazy with it.

Donovan catches my mouth in his, and it grounds me. I

secure myself in his lips, anchoring myself to him. His tongue slides against mine, tasting me, and I shiver.

"All these years," Donovan muses, "and you two still make me see stars."

I laugh at that. "Some things never change, do they?"

"No. They don't."

We break apart but come together again. The three of us snuggle in bed together, Donovan wedged in between both Jason and me. The both of us are starved for his body, trapping him in with us. I rest my head against his chest. My husband. My partner in crime. My pain in the ass.

My Donovan.

Our Donovan.

I rest my hand on his hip. My thumb rubs against that familiar scar, the place where he sacrificed part of himself to save our son.

The backs of my eyes burn. "I love our family," I say suddenly, because I have to say it.

Donovan chuckles lightly. He presses the top of my head. "Me too."

"Muskrats forever," Jason adds. He winds his arms around the both of us and pulls us into a tight hug. I don't want to be anywhere else.

26

DIEGO

"Otto! Your dad is live!"

Naomi shouts the announcement. Otto and I are already in my bed when she bounces out of the bathroom, toothbrush in her mouth, and plops her body between us.

"I sure hope he's alive, or this is going to be a shitty New Year," Otto replies.

"No, he's LU-iiiive."

Naomi holds up her phone so we can see the screen. It shows Jason's social profile with a bouncing circle around his picture, noting that he's filming a live video for his followers.

"Are you following him?" Otto asks.

Naomi blushes. "Hush and watch."

She clicks the video, and it starts to play.

Jason finishes adjusting his camera. He's wearing slacks and a partially buttoned shirt. His hair is slightly teased, like he's had one (or more) hands running through it. I don't know if Otto's dad is fully aware of what a "thirst trap" he is, but it certainly doesn't hurt his brand.

I know their house as well as I know my own, and he's definitely not at home—he's sitting at a table with a large window in the background. Through the window, there's a beautiful view of the ocean and sky.

Where the hell is he that's *that* high up?

He starts speaking, and my questions dissolve on my tongue.

"Hey, King Squad," he says. His smile is lopsided, his voice low. "Apologies for whispering. My others are, uh…sleeping. I hope you're all settled in with your chosen family of the day. I don't want to take up too much of your time, but I did want to follow up with something.

"I've talked a lot this year about letting go. Moving on. But we can't move on from the things we don't acknowledge. Earlier this year, we lost a member of our chosen family. Maria. She was a good friend, a great mom, and her son and our son grew up together.

"I'm going to leave you with a memory that our son is going to kill me for."

("Please don't be the Chatham story," Otto mumbles.)

"So we're taking a weekend trip to Chatham—"

("*Fuck,*" Otto groans.)

"—Kenzi, Donovan, and I sailed out on *Dock Buoy*, and we brought Maria and her son, Diego, along with us. Otto and Diego were fifteen or sixteen, maybe, and Joan was just a puppy. The boys were getting cabin fever, so we let them take the dinghy to shore to play on the beach. Thought nothing of it, right? Well, never underestimate the power of teenage boys. They got the idea to take this little motorized boat for a joyride and got themselves beached on a sandbar.

"Luckily, we had a kayak with us, so Maria and I take the kayak and paddle out to the boys. They're hangdog, you know, *we'll never do it again*, blah, blah. So Maria and I get in the dinghy, and we find out that not only have they beached it, but they've punctured the hull and now there's about an inch of water in the thing.

"We get the boys in the kayak and try to figure out what

to do with the dinghy. So I'm hunting around for something to plug it up with, and Maria looks at me and she goes, *Hold on to something.*

"Then she guns the motor. The funny thing about these little boats—if you make them go fast enough, the boat hydroplanes, so all the water it'd collected drained out the back. So Maria practically breaks the sound barrier and zips this thing across the bay and beaches it on a private beach.

"There are two times I've feared for my life. That was one of them. Luckily, everyone made it out in one piece. We had to swim back to the boat, but in good news, we didn't have to drag the bay for a sunken dinghy.

"That's it. That's my favorite Maria story. She was a brave, strong, and take-no-shit woman. I haven't mentioned Maria because…it's hard for me to talk about her. It's hard for me to be sad. It's hard for me to let the people around me suffer in grief. I want so badly to fix things and make them right. But people are complicated. Grief isn't always a bad thing. Sometimes it's just…an expression of love.

"So—I know my big line is *cut out negativity*. But this year…maybe don't be afraid to lean into the part of you that feels uncomfortable. The bruises are still there, and ignoring them isn't going to heal them quicker. If I have one sweeping holiday wish for myself…it's to spend this season surrounded by love. Love each other. Love yourself. Love when it feels good. Love when it hurts. Just love.

"Okay. That's all. Love you all. Happy holidays."

With that, Jason gives the camera a smile and then reaches forward and presses his finger to the screen, and the video cuts.

There's a knot in my throat the size of the *Titanic*.

I can feel their eyes on me.

"Hey…" Naomi says tenderly. "Are you okay?"

"Uh-huh."

But I can barely get the noise out. The backs of my eyes are burning.

I hide my face in my hands. A half sob escapes, and immediately, Naomi and Otto descend. Otto's arms wrap around my middle, and Naomi strokes a hand through my hair, pulling me against her chest.

"Sorry," I say.

"It's okay," she murmurs.

"I know…" My voice breaks, pent-up emotions struggling to come out. "It's…uh. These are happy tears. Not sad." I sniff and try to straighten out. I push the heels of my hands against my eyes, keeping my tears at bay. "It meant a lot to hear that."

"Your mom sounded like a badass," Naomi murmurs.

"Yeah." I grin. "She was."

For a moment, the three of us lapse into silence. It feels good just to be held by them.

I feel safe here. Supported.

It's okay to let myself be weak in this moment when I have the both of them here to prop me up.

Finally, Otto says, "I know exactly what will make us feel better."

PART VI

NEW YEARS' DAY. JANUARY 1

27

OTTO

*J*anuary first. Start of a New Year.

The start of new habits. The creation of new futures. The great, big, unknown *new year, new me*.

But it's also a good time to pay respect to the old traditions that have kept you afloat all of these years.

Even if I'm the only one enjoying myself. Naomi sits on the picnic bench beside me, shivering. "Tell me again why we're sitting outside an ice cream shop...*in the middle of winter?*"

I shrug. "It's tradition."

"You couldn't pick a warmer tradition?"

"Blame is on Dad J," Joan says. "He's the ice cream fanatic."

"Jason and Otto's first hangout happened at this ice cream shop," Diego says, filling in the blanks. "They've been doing a family picture every winter since."

"Awww," Naomi coos and bats her eyes at me. "More baby stories, please."

I make a face at her. "No."

The four of us sit on a picnic bench outside Hannsett Island's local ice cream shop, *Ahoy!* The shop hasn't changed in decades—it still has the same cheap, wooden benches, the same cartoon whale drawing on its large sign. There's a thin coating of snow on most of the tables, but we brushed it off this one to wait. The seats are cold, but the morning sun is warm on our backs. Naomi sits next to me, Diego and Joan across from us.

Joan is stuffed in a beaten leather jacket, and she picks at the sleeves. She leaves to head back to London next week. I want to soak up all the time I have with my little sister before she's gone.

Even if she won't be far. Part of her rests inside of me, still healing, still slowly making itself at home with the rest of me.

"Do you want my jacket?" Diego offers Naomi.

She shakes her head. "I just want to complain."

I unbutton my coat and open a side, holding it out like a wing. She crawls inside my coat, half sitting on my lap.

Just then, my parents' car pulls into the parking lot. I give Naomi's side a squeeze. "Incoming."

My parents exit the car. Everyone is wearing the same clothes they wore last night.

Okay, I see you.

Jason is wearing dark shades, but he takes them off and hooks them on his sweater when he approaches us. He extends his arms out wide, a big grin on his lips.

"The whole gang is here!"

"Duh," Joan says.

I shrug. "It's tradition."

Jason beams. You have never seen a happier man. It makes my heart warm to see him this way.

Mom and Donovan catch up to the rest of us. They have their hands linked together.

"Alright," Jason says. "What's everyone want? Kenz? Mint?"

We're a horde when we go to the ice cream counter. It takes ten minutes just to get through everyone's ice cream orders. I get a cup of coffee-flavored, and Naomi and Diego both steal large scoops of ice cream.

I've finally found the downside to polyamory. Too much food sharing.

We all settle back down on the picnic table outside. Mom gets Joan to talk a little bit about her adventures in London. Donovan and Diego discuss the hospital. Naomi straight-up steels the rest of my ice cream, and we trade cups.

Joan, who is at that age where she can only stand her parents for a couple of minutes at a time, starts to get ornery halfway through her cone.

She groans loudly at one of Jason's bad jokes, and Jason squints at her. "What's up? Your ice cream too hot? Need me to blow on it?"

He blows on her ice cream. Even moody Joan bursts into chuckles at that.

My heart tightens in my chest.

Fuck. I love these people.

I need to immortalize this moment.

"Alright," I announce and take my phone out of my coat pocket. "Picture time."

Diego holds out his hand. "I can take it."

"Don't be an idiot. It's a *family* photo. You're family."

Diego opens his mouth to protest but then catches himself. A little grin appears on his mouth instead. "Okay," he says.

Good boy.

I tap a young woman on her shoulder. "Hey—can you take a picture of us?"

She holds up the phone, aiming the camera toward us.

She snaps a flurry of photos. When I go through them later, I discover they're all *ridiculous*.

In one, Naomi is cross-eyed, and Jason is licking Donovan's face.

In another, Joan has me in a chokehold.

In another, Mom is doubled over, laughing so hard that she drops her ice cream on the ground.

The last is quasi-decent. My arm around Diego's chest. Naomi's head on my shoulder. Jason, Kenzi, and Donovan holding Joan in their arms like a princess.

All of us, smiling. Happy. *In love.*

I print this photo out and tuck it into the first page of my new notebook. I want to be reminded every time I open it: I'm grateful every day I get to love and be loved by these bizarre humans.

And I wouldn't have it any other way.

THE END

* * *

Note from Adora: Thank you for reading "All I Want For Christmas is Them," my third installment in the "Truth or Dare" series!

I hope you had as much fun with these characters as I did. If so, please consider leaving a review — it means so much to hear what you think.

If you'd like to stay up to date on my next releases, you can sign up to get newsletter alerts (plus you get a free MMF romance).

Join the club ➤ https://adoracrooksbooks.com/gift

XOXO,

Adora

ABOUT THE AUTHOR

USA Today bestselling author Adora Crooks writes romance with heart, action, humor, and steam. She is a sucker for kick-ass heroines and the strong, brooding men who crave them (and sometimes crave each other, too).

A former New Yorker, she currently resides in the magical city of New Orleans with her beloved and their two nutty mutts. Adora lives off of coffee, cookies, and book reviews and daydreams about dirty romances with happy-ever-afters.

Join her newsletter to download a free romance ➡ https://adoracrooksbooks.com/gift

THE TRUTH OR DARE SERIES

Truth or Dare (The Complete Duet)

The Bully's Dare + The Doctor's Truth + Two Truth & A Lie all in one collection (Paperback available)

Book 1: The Bully's Dare

At 18, Kenzi spends the summer with her mom in a small island off the coast of Long Island. But when she loses her v-card to her two best friends, things get complicated.

Book 2: The Doctor's Truth

Kenzi is a single mom with a big secret…her son, Otto. When Otto gets sick, she has to go back to the place she ran from…and the two men she ran from.

Book 2.5: Two Truths & A Lie

Jason is recently divorced, and he needs somewhere to stay. Donovan invites him home. Can they navigate living together or will things get…hard?

Book 3: All I Want For Christmas Is Them

Otto is all grown up…and he's spending Christmas with his girlfriend, Naomi, and his best friend, Diego.

Spin Off: Doctor All Nighter

Ash's playboy next door neighbor is keeping her up…all night. If you can't beat them, join them, right? Except her one-night stand turns into a lifetime commitment, and her OBGYN is the very neighbor who put the baby inside of her.

Not officially part of the Truth or Dare Series, but Donovan does make an appearance as the MC's coworker & friend.

ALSO BY ADORA CROOKS

MMF Ménage & LGBTQ+ Romance

The Royal's Love (Complete Series)

Rory is a lone American vlogging her way through England. When she goes home with the attractive stranger from the bar, she doesn't expect him to be the prince's bodyguard…or for the prince to join in. When their menage a trois goes viral, sh*t really hits the fan.

Mr. Hollywood's Secret

Eric North is Hollywood's favorite leading man. But he has a secret: his boyfriend, Nico. When his agent sets him up with a fake fiancee, the chemistry between all three of them is very real.

M/F Romance

The Best Man Wins

She's a wedding planner with her career on the line. He's the best man determined to break up the engagement before the couple says their vows. It's a battle to the final "I do."

Protecting His Finch

She's trapped as the ward of a mafia family. He's the older bodyguard who has protected her for years. Can they escape the family and find peace together?